The

Partners

©2022

1

I

Dave Bristol was just beginning his sixteenth year patrolling the streets of Cincinnati. Because of his seniority, he was able to pick the District he worked in, the shift and the beat. Dave liked District One, which serves the downtown area. He also liked working alone because it forced him to be cautious and he did not feel the need to impress someone else.

Robin Milner had eight years on the job and enjoyed being in District Five, which covers the area around the University of Cincinnati campus. At five feet four inches and one hundred and twenty pounds, she had to prove herself to bad guys on a regular basis. She worked the evening shift and liked the action because the shift went quickly.

Robin arrived for her shift and found a note in her pigeon hole waiting for her. It announced that, effective the next Sunday, she was being transferred to District One on the two p.m. to midnight shift. Robin was pissed as she loved the officers that she got to work with, but this was not something she had any control over.

Dave arrived for his shift on Sunday and the Sergeant motioned him into the supervisor's office. Sgt. Terry Martin closed the office door and told Dave that his beat had been amended to be a two person car and that he would introduce Dave to his new partner. Dave groaned and started to say something when the Sergeant placed his finger to his lips and waived the finger back and forth.

The Sergeant said, "This was not my idea. It came directly from the Captain and there is nothing to negotiate. It is going to happen." The two walked out into the roll call room and the Sergeant introduced him to Officer Milner.

The tension between the two was clear and apparent. At six feet two inches and two hundred and ten pounds, the pair looked like Mutt and Jeff standing next to each other. They sat through the roll call and then went to gather the equipment they would need for the shift. They agreed that each would take turns driving with each driving for a week. Dave told Robin that she could take the first week.

They loaded the patrol vehicle with the shotgun and tactical rifle without exchanging any words. Robin pulled out of the parking lot and headed toward their beat when they received a call to a bar fight at the Walnut Café on Ninth Street downtown.

Robin pulled the cruiser up near the front door and was out of the car before Dave had the passenger door open. She walked up to the entrance, which was blocked by a large male, who was not going to allow her to pass. Dave had just gotten out of the cruiser when he heard the male say, "Go back to your sewing little bitch." Dave was still walking toward the door when he saw Robin drive her fingers into the chest of the man causing him to gasp and crumple to the ground. She then stepped over him and walked into the bar. As Dave stepped over the male, he said, "Attempt to get up and I promise you will leave here in an ambulance."

Dave entered the bar and saw Robin with a vice grip on a male's penis. She ordered the male to place his hands behind his back as he was under arrest. The male, who was on his tippy-toes, quicky complied. Dave placed one handcuff on and realized that the prisoner was a body builder and had no flexibility in his arms. Dave told Robin to give him her handcuffs and hooked the two sets together to get the prisoner secured. Only when the handcuffs were in place, did Robin release her grip. Three more cops walked into the bar just after she let go of his manhood and heard the sigh of relief as the man was no longer in pain. One of the cops asked Dave, "What is the story of the guy on the ground outside?" Dave smiled and answered, "Go out and tell him to hit the road." Dave turned the prisoner so Robin could grab the handcuffs and she marched him out the front door. Dave opened the back door of the cruiser and stepped back so Robin could get the prisoner into the cruiser. She pushed the guy's head down and then guided him into the cruiser, slamming the door shut. They drove to the Hamilton County Justice Center and Robin pushed the trunk release so that they could put their firearms into it. Firearms are prohibited inside of the jail.

When they got inside, the sheriff's deputy working intake smiled and said, "You always bring us new friends Robin." Looking at Dave, the deputy said, "Robin is one of our favorite city cops. She keeps us busy."

After getting their handcuffs back, the two completed the arrest slip and signed the complaints to get the prisoner into the system. While they were completing the paperwork Dave asked, "By the way, what are we arresting this moron for?" Robin looked up from the paper and said, "He pushed me after telling me, "Go away little girl."

They returned to the cruiser and retrieved their weapons. Dave said, "Let's pick up our coffee." They sat in the cruiser watching the giant steel door open to the street when communications broadcast an aggravated robbery less than one block from the Justice Center. They saw a black male running westbound on Ninth Street with a gun in his right hand and a brown bag in his left. The door opened and Dave jumped out of the car to give chase while Robin got on the radio to broadcast the foot pursuit. The chase ran southwest through two parking lots onto Eighth Street when the eighteen year old suspect ran south into an alley that had a ten foot high cement wall. The kid jumped on a plastic bucket at the base of the wall using it as a springboard to get over the wall. Since the bucket was kicked over, Dave would have to replace it and then get a running start to repeat the process. Dave notified communications that he lost the suspect over the wall when he heard Robin say, "Car 1204A, I have one at gunpoint 135 East Seventh Street."

Dave ran back the way he came in and ran full speed around the block to get to his partner. When he turned the corner, there were already four cops there and the suspect was in handcuffs. The gun he was carrying was shoved inside her belt. Communications called and told the pair to take the suspect to the Criminal Investigation Section office so he could be interviewed by detectives. When they took the prisoner into CIS, Robin told the detectives they would be back in an hour to transport him to the jail.

The two then drove to Frisch's restaurant and spent the next hour enjoying their dinner. They were still off the air with the prisoner and were not available for calls. Dave asked how she knew where the suspect would over the wall. She smiled and answered, "I did a stint with Central Vice Unit and that it was the method the drug dealers would use to get away. I smiled when he dropped to the ground and said, "MAKE MY DAY!" Dave laughed hard when he heard that.

They returned to CIS and picked up the prisoner. All of the necessary paperwork was completed by the detectives, so all they had to do was drop him off and get their handcuffs back. When they brought the prisoner into the Intake, the deputy looked at Robin and said, "Took you long enough to get back here. You slacking again?"

Dave wanted to show her the 'hot spots' on the beat, so he pointed things out as they drove the streets. They were sitting at the light at Court and Broadway when a car blew by them against the light. Dave activated the overhead lights and tapped on the siren to get the driver to pull over. After two blocks, the Toyota Camry pulled to the right side of the street and stopped. Dave entered the license plate number into the Mobil Digital Computer and the screen flashed that the vehicle was reported stolen. Robin walked up the driver side of the car while Dave went up the passenger side. When Dave looked in the passenger window, he saw something silver flash into his view. Dave yelled "GUN" and drew his firearm while opening the passenger door and grabbing the passenger by the collar and depositing him on the pavement. He could now see a nickel plated .32 caliber semi-automatic laying on the floor. Robin brought the driver out of the car at gunpoint as well. She was putting handcuffs on him when police cars converged to help them. They put the prisoners into the cruiser and then went back to search the interior of the Toyota. Under the driver's seat they found a brown bag with individually packaged cream colored rocks that appeared to be crack cocaine. There were also several pills in the bag which they could not identify. Robin asked one of the other officers to babysit the car until the wrecker arrived so they could take the suspects back to the District.

Once at the District, Dave called for a Street Corner Unit officer, the street level drug unit, to help them identify the pills. They used a Physician's Desk Reference book to match the drugs to the pictures in the book and then signed all of the evidence into the District property room. After that, they took the two down to the Justice Center.

While driving back to call it a day Dave said, "Been a long while since I have had that much fun in a single shift. Two guns, four prisoners and multiple felonies. Thanks for the great shift."

Dave walked into the locker room and up to his locker to put his duty belt in the locker. He glanced back and saw Robin standing a few feet away. He smiled and said, "You do know that this is the MEN'S LOCKER ROOM, don't you?"? Robin looked directly into his eyes and said, "Take off all of your clothes." Dave got a befuddled look on his face but slowly removed his shirt, bullet proof vest, and tee shirt. The he dropped his pants showing that he was not wearing any underwear. He stood naked for a moment and then watched as Robin removed her shirt, vest and sports bra and then dropped her pants showing that she wore no panties either. There was a moment of silence and Robin said, "Now we have seen all of each other and we can just go about doing our job." She dressed quickly and walked out of the locker room.

II

Robin walked into the District for the start of the shift and was informed that Dave had put in a slip to take the first two hours off to work security at a Cincinnati Reds baseball game. She was used to working alone, so she patrolled her beat without any incident.

After the game was over, Dave called Police Communications by phone and told the operator to dispatch Car 1204 to pick up her partner in front of Great American Ball Park. Less than five minutes later Robin pulled up and Dave jumped into the passenger seat. He suggested they pick up coffee before things got busy. After stopping at a United Dairy Farmers, Robin pulled into a parking lot on Ninth Street so they could drink their coffee. Dave told Robin, "The reason that I need to work off duty details is that I have three children in Catholic schools and the tuitions put a stress on my base salary. This allows my wife to be a stay-at-home mom.

Robin nodded her head in agreement and told Dave. "I leave my badge and gun on a table at home when I am not working. My partner is an emergency room physician at St. Elizabeth Hospital and she works sixteen hour shifts. She has a room at the hospital with a bed in it and they wake her if she is needed. Our time together is so limited that I just want to forget that I am a cop and be with her."

They completed their coffee and just tossed the cups into a trash container when a call came out advising a bank robbery at the Huntington Bank at Seventh and Vine. The getaway car was last seen turning onto Ninth Street heading toward the Interstate. The broadcast was not finished when Robin yelled out, "There it goes!" At almost the same time the cops saw the vehicle, the driver saw the cruiser and sped away.

Dave activated the overhead lights and siren and called the pursuit into Communications. The vehicle continued on Ninth Street and jumped onto Interstate 75 northbound, increasing its speed to over ninety miles per hour. Dave cautioned Robin that northbound would clog due to rush hour and to be cautious. The chase went up the Interstate through Saint Bernard where one of their units joined. Traffic started to clog and the suspects took to the emergency lane until they reached the Norwood Lateral, which is a limited access road that runs from I-75 to I-71. Norwood Police had two units join in and they got onto Interstate 71 northbound. The Sheriff's Department and Ohio Highway Patrol joined the chase which continued north for several miles as they left Hamilton County and entered Warren County. A state patrol car pulled even with Robin and put on his right blinker indicating that he wanted to take the lead. Robin backed off and the state cruiser slid in. Ohio Highway Patrol is one of the few agencies in Ohio that trains their officers in the P.I.T. maneuver. The Parallel Intervention Technique uses the front quarter panel of the cruiser to nudge the rear quarter panel of the pursued vehicle causing it to go into a spin. The state trooper tapped the right rear quarter panel of the pursued car causing it to rotate and go into the grass median. A Warren County Sheriff's cruiser then slammed into the rear of the car. A state cruiser blocked the front of the bad guy's car and a Montgomery Police unit pushed against the driver door, leaving only the passenger door available for an exit. Cops surrounded the car armed with tactical rifles, shotguns and pistols and brought the four men out one at a time. Robin and Dave handcuffed the first two and took them to their cruiser and the other two were placed in an OSP cruiser. The two cars drove all the way back to District One headquarters where two FBI agents were waiting. They announced that the four men would be charged with Federal bank robbery charges as they were also wanted for robberies in Indianapolis, Indiana, Louisville and Lexington, Kentucky. They called the United States Marshals for transportation to the Boone County, Kentucky Jail because it was the closest jail with a contract to house Federal prisoners.

By the time the prisoners were removed, the shift was over. Dave walked into the locker room and stopped at his locker, this time turning around to see that no one was in there.

***

Dave woke up early so that he could get some yard work done. After he was done, he made a sandwich and sat down in front of the television to watch the noon local news. The lead story was the start of a Murder trial in the killing of an elderly woman found in her kitchen near the University of Cincinnati campus. The news showed the testimony of the State's first witness, Robin, who captured the suspect. She testified that she was the first officer to arrive and found the dead woman. She saw the rear door standing open and, when she went into the back yard, she

11

saw footprints in the wet grass. She followed the footprints through the yards of two homes when she saw the defendant hiding under a porch with a gun in his right hand. She ordered the man to come out, but he refused. She called for a canine and the dog crawled under the porch and bit the man in the buttock. The man let out a yell and crawled out from under the porch leaving the weapon under the porch. She testified that she called for a rescue unit because the man was bleeding from the bite and handcuffed him. She went on to say that she rode in the ambulance with the prisoner to University of Cincinnati Medical Center. While in route to the hospital, the defendant told her that he broke into to the house to steal money to buy drugs and that the woman's entry caused him to panic. The defense attorney jumped out of his chair to object, telling the judge that the officer had not made any statement that she had advised the defendant of his right to remain silent. The judge looked at Robin and asked, "Officer, did you inform the defendant of his rights?" Robin answered, "No sir, I did not. I had no intention, and did not ask any questions. He made the statement voluntarily and without and questioning from me." The judge overruled the objection stating that the statement was an 'excited utterance' and was admissible. When it was his turn to cross examine, the defense attorney asked Robin, "You testified that my client was in possession of a firearm. Why didn't you shoot him if he had a gun?" Robin answered, "He never pointed the weapon in my direction, so there was never a threat that would lead to use lethal force."

When Dave arrived at the District, he was informed that Robin was in court and would not be returning to work until Monday. He spent the next two shifts working alone and had two very dull shifts.

***

When the two walked into the roll call room, they were greeted by a cop yelling, "We are blessed to have the presence of the Dynamic Duo, Batman and Robin are here." There was an immediate response of catcalls and whoops. One cop walked over to Robin and asked, "Can I please get your autograph?" In a soft but stern voice Robin said, "How would you like me to rip off your nuts and hand them to you?" The cop quickly retreated to a chair in the other side of the room.

The Sergeant handed Dave and Robin a photograph of a male wanted for homicide. The man had a girlfriend who lived in a second floor apartment on Court Street. After getting their coffee, Dave drove to a parking lot on Court Street where they could see the apartment building. They had only been there about twenty minutes when the man walked out of the building. Robin jumped out of the cruiser just as the man saw the police car. He ran to the street and jumped into a car which took off at a high rate of speed. Dave stopped long enough to pick up Robin and gave chase. The car turned south on Plum Street until it ran out of road at the Convention Center. It turned west on Sixth Street and then south on Central Avenue. When it reached the Ohio River, the two men got out and ran, jumping into the Ohio River. Both cops laughed as they watched the two morons flounder around in the river.

Dave called Communications and requested the Fire Department Duck. The Duck is an amphibious vehicle which can operate on the street or in the water. When it arrived, the cops got on and rode as it entered the river. The firemen got the suspects out of the water where the cops put them in handcuffs. When they got back on dry land, they moved the two men to the cruiser and transported them to the Justice Center. They opened the trunk to deposit their weapons before moving the suspects into the jail. Once inside, a deputy looked at Robin and said, "We like you. What did we do to you that you would bring these stinky toads here? Now we have to get them a shower before we can take them upstairs," Robin smiled and said, "You do not have to live with the stench that our cruiser has for six hours, quit bitching."

They left the jail and drove to a car wash to vacuum out the back seat. Dave bought air freshener to spray in the back seat and they waited fifteen minutes before getting back into the car. They were thrilled that the smell had dissipated.

They decided to stop at Arnold's for their dinner meal. Arnold's is a bar that is across the street from the Hamilton County Justice center and serves home cooked meals. They were eating when Robin asked, "Why didn't you ever take the Sergeant's exam, you would make a great boss? Dave munched on his meat loaf and then replied, "That is a fair question that deserves an honest answer. I could not take the cut in pay. I would lose almost all of my extra duty details and almost all of the court time which pays time and a half because I am maxed out on compensatory time. The City has to pay me at overtime. I made Police Specialist four years ago, which was a seven percent pay raise and did not affect any of my detail money. When my kids are done with school and my age precludes me from being in the action every day, I will likely start to look at the pay increase. I enjoy playing in the sandbox too much now to be a boss and spend all my time writing paper."

The radio cracked out a police officer needs assistance in the projects and the two cops jumped out of their seats, each throwing a twenty dollar bill at the cashier. Dave got behind the wheel while Robin activated the lights and siren. They were about halfway to the address when the call to disregard was broadcast. Like most cops, they ignored the cancellation and continued at full speed to the scene. When they arrived, they saw cruisers parked in the grass, on the sidewalk and in all directions on the road. They got of the car and could see three males laying on their stomachs in the grass. Dave walked up to a young cop who was bleeding from the nose and asked, "What the hell happened?" The cop answered, "I was trying to arrest the goober in the middle for open warrants when the monkey on the right roundhoused me. I think he broke my nose. The joker on the left also has warrants. Dave said, "Do you need a ride to the hospital to get checked out?" The young cop said, "I have to stay here until a boss arrives so he can take pictures of my pretty face and get pictures of the three morons to prove that we did not tune them up. Someone already called a rescue unit for me."

The two cops turned around and walked back to their cruiser. As they arrived, they watched a Lieutenant get out of a cruiser with a camera and heard the siren of the ambulance.

As they returned to their beat, Dave asked, "So why aren't you a Sergeant, you have the time in to get there?" Robin groaned and said, "You deserve an honest answer as well. I failed both the Sergeant and Police Specialist tests because I was too lazy to study for them. I know that I would have gotten promoted if I had simply passed because of the matrix of being on the secondary list of minority officers, who get promoted without scoring at the top. I will take them next opportunity and actually study the material in the test."

Dave said, "I have had offers to join canine, traffic section, and investigator, but have turned them all down because I like being a street cop."

The shift ended without any further incidents.

***

The two were driving across Ninth Street headed toward the Queensgate business district when Dave saw a vehicle driving westbound. He entered the license plate into the mobile computer and told Robin, "Something about this car isn't right, I want to make a traffic stop." The car was registered to a fifty-one year old man with no criminal record.

The car immediately pulled over when the overhead lights were turned on. The car stopped on the Eighth Street

Viaduct which goes over rail yards and connects the west side to the downtown district. The two could only see a grey haired white male in the driver's seat.

Robin started toward the driver's door when Dave looked at the vehicle and saw the driver staring at the outside mirror. He immediately grabbed Robin's shoulder and pulled her backward causing her to fall to the ground. Seconds later the vehicle exploded in a ball of fire and parts of the car spread out for one hundred yards. Robin looked up with a quizzical glance and Dave said. "I saw him checking the side mirror and his face told me something was about to happen."

Dave called for fire, a supervisor and homicide to respond to the scene and asked that the viaduct be shut down on both sides. In less than two minutes Dave could see three marked police cars blocking the area behind and the flashing of police lights at the other end.

A fire truck pulled up and began spraying water on the vehicle without much success. A second pumper worked diligently to extinguish the flames which fully engulfed the car. It took a few minutes for the fire to be put out and they could then see the charred remains of the driver in the front seat.

A sergeant pulled up and immediately asked what the hell was happening. Dave explained the situation just as the two homicide detectives arrived.

When the detectives cleared the scene, they obtained a search warrant for the man's home where they found the materials used to make the incendiary device and a handwritten note indicating that the man intended to commit suicide because he was despondent over the death of his mother.

III

Dave and Robin sat in the roll call listening to the boring reports from the previous shifts and were glad to get out into the street. They drove from the District across Central Parkway onto Sycamore Street passing the Justice Center. As they crossed Eighth Street, they watched a young male grab a woman's purse and run south. Dave gunned the cruiser forward until they caught up to the runner and then stopped to let Robin out. She chased the suspect and Dave saw the two enter a three story apartment building. Dave stood at the corner of Seventh and Sycamore and called for more cars to surround the building. Dave heard a scream and then watched as a male dropped from the roof of the building splitting like a pumpkin when he hit the asphalt of the alley. He looked up at the roof, but saw nothing. A few minutes later, Robin walked out of the front door holding the woman's purse in her hand. She walked over to Dave and said, "See, I told you that I knew my limitations."

Dave called for a supervisor, homicide and the coroner and told Robin, "You know that the headhunters are going to want to ask you if you helped him over the edge." Robin answered, "Yea, I know, but I was ten feet behind him when he tried to make the other roof. He missed by about a foot." The Sergeant arrived and looked at the young man, who spilled a lot of blood into the alley. He looked at Robin and said, "You might want an FOP lawyer with you."

After finally convincing the investigators that she did not push the suspect off the roof, the two went back on patrol. Dave said, "I am hosting a cookout this Saturday at my home. There will be a few select cops and my family attending. Love to have you come and bring your partner. It will be an opportunity for you to meet my family as well. Robin sat quietly for a moment and then said, "I have never introduced my partner to any cops before." Dave answered, "Many of the cops bring their significant other and this is a very low key event. You should come."

Robin and Elaine arrived in front of Dave's home to find his driveway full of cars and most of the street parking taken. They walked up to a fence leading to the rear yard and opened the gate where they were met by a large brown german shepherd. The dog walked up and sniffed both of them causing Robin to yell "DAVE!." A few moments later Dave rounded the corner and said, "General, off." The dog slowly turned and walked into the back yard. Dave laughed and said, "Great dog. If we are home, you can beat on him and poke his eyes out without fear. If we are not home, he will shred you like pulled pork."

The three walked into the back yard where a large grill was already smoking with hot dogs, hamburgers, and German bratts and metts. On a table was an array of potato salad, baked beans, pasta salad and potato chips covered with plastic. Robin noticed that people walking in were each bringing a dish for the guests. She looked at Dave and said, "I wish you had told me to bring something, I feel terrible." Dave smiled and replied, "First visit is on the house, bring something to the next one."

Dave took the two over to a woman and two young men and a young woman and said, "This is my wife Cheryl and my three children, Dave, Jr., Marcie and William. This is my new partner Robin and her partner whose name I don't know yet." Robin blushed and said, "This is Elaine, a doctor at St. Elizabeth Hospital, nice to meet you."

Robin and Elaine walked around the back yard introducing themselves to cops that Robin did not know. One older cop looked at Robin and said, "So this is the other half of Batman and Robin that I keep hearing about. I wonder how they came up with that name!"

Elaine looked uncomfortable in the setting, but Dave kept coming over and telling her to relax and enjoy saying, "No one here bites." There was music playing on the radio loudly and Robin and Elaine ate and enjoyed the relaxed atmosphere of the event. They stayed a couple of hours before returning home. They smiled at Dave and thanked him for the invitation, promising to bring dessert the next time.

After the ladies left, Dave's wife walked up to Dave and said, "Robin is a very pretty lady. Do I need to be worried?" Dave laughed and answered, "The woman with Robin is the love of her life. I don't have the right biological equipment to interest her."

After Robin and Dave sat down in the roll call room, Robin said, "Thank you for the hospitality at your cookout. It was the first time I introduced Elaine to cops and she had a positive experience. I hope you will invite us back."

They walked out to their cruiser as the radio cracked out a person shot in the West End. They arrived at the scene and found a teenager laying in the grass who had been shot in the head and was dead. A witness told them that a young boy was the shooter and ran east toward the project. Robin put out the description over the air and they secured the scene waiting for the forensic team and the homicide dicks to arrive. They located the shell casings from a nine millimeter in the gutter near the street and located a security camera that likely caught the incident on video. They relayed that to the two homicide investigators and remained at the scene until the investigators collected everything they needed. The victim was only sixteen years old and his mother had to be restrained because she tried her best to forcibly get to her child.

They were driving west on Ninth Street when a call came out for a car crash with injuries on Interstate 75 northbound. When they arrived at the scene, they saw two cars smoking in what appeared to be a head-on crash. The Interstate was closed to allow a medical helicopter to land to airlift a man and woman in the car traveling northbound. A young cop walked up to Robin and said, "We have an issue we need help with. There was a four year old child in a car seat in the rear of the vehicle with the man and woman. He was unhurt because he was secured in the seat, but is crying uncontrollably. Can you help him?" Robin ran over to the child and grabbed him hugging him tightly. She softly whispered in his ear and, after a minute, the child stopped crying. He wrapped his arms around Robin's neck and held on with a death grip. Robin carried the child to their cruiser and told Dave to retrieve the car seat from the car so they could take him to the hospital to be with his parents. Dave put the car seat on the hood of the cruiser and Robin attempted to put the boy into it. The child tightened his grip on her neck and began crying again. Robin looked at Dave and said, "I guess he will be riding in the front seat with me. Put the car seat in the cruiser." They were in no hurry to get to the hospital, so there was no need to use the lights and siren. Once inside University of Cincinnati Medical Center, they were escorted to a surgical waiting room. Dave left the waiting room to get them coffee and Robin sat on a couch holding the child who fell asleep on her shoulder. When Dave returned, Robin tried to put the child on the couch, but he would have no part of it. They sat in the waiting room as the child slept for almost two hours when a nurse walked into the room and said, "I am sorry, but neither of the parents survived the surgery. Our staff was able to locate the female's brother and he is in route here now. Robin sipped on her coffee with one hand while the other held the child. It was just over an hour later when a man and woman entered the waiting room. The child immediately recognized his uncle and put his arms out for the uncle to hold him. Now it was Robin who did not want to release her grip on the boy. Dave walked over and patted her on the back saying, "It's okay to let him go." As the boy was being exchanged between the two, he leaned back and kissed Robin on the cheek. As the two cops left the area, Dave could see Robin's eyes welling up with tears. They got into the cruiser and Robin said, "That is the first time I have cried since I was fourteen!" Dave smiled weakly and responded, "It is okay for us to have feelings.

We did not give them up just because we are cops." The rest of the night went quietly and little was said between the two.

***

The next few months came and went with nothing of interest. The one positive was that the two partners solidified their bond. One knew what the other would do and they had total trust in each other.

They had just gotten into their cruiser to start their shift when Robin turned on the computer. She saw a call to the Kroger store to pick up a shoplifter being held in the manager's office. The two walked into the Manager's office and saw a nineteen year old woman sitting in a chair crying. Dave put on the handcuffs and Robin inquired as to what the woman stole. The manager pointed to a plastic bag of diapers. The three walked out of the store onto the sidewalk when Robin said, "I need to go back into the store, I will be right back." She walked into the store and found the manager. She asked him if twenty dollars would cover the cost of the diapers. The manager nodded his head and Robin reached into her pocket and pulled out a twenty dollar bill. She told the manager, "Now there is no crime," picked up the diapers and walked out of the store. She told Dave to remove the handcuffs and handed the woman the diapers. She said, "They are paid for. There is no crime. You are free to leave." The young woman took the diapers and briskly walked away. Dave laughed and said, "She did not even say thank you." Robin looked at Dave and answered, "I don't think she had time to think about anything other than getting the hell outta here."

They had just gotten back into the cruiser when the radio cracked, "Attention District One cars, Shot Spotter indicates multiple shots fired Thirteenth and Pendleton." They were the first unit on the scene and saw three males on the ground. They jumped out of the car and immediately smelled the stench of urine and fecal waste, indicating that the males were dead. At death the muscles relax releasing all bodily fluids. Dave would later tell Robin about witnessing an officer shoot a suspect. When the suspect died, his urine shot up through his pants like a fountain. Dave said it was the scariest thing he had ever seen. Dave moved the cruiser to block the intersection while Robin put in a call for the Coroner, Homicide and the Forensic Unit to respond. Other cruisers arrived and shut down the area while Robin put up crime scene tape. A Lieutenant arrived and told Robin to monitor the traffic and told Dave to assist the crime scene techs to help locate evidence.

Thirty-four casings were located on both sides of the street indicating that there were at least two shooters in a moving vehicle. The 9mm rounds were likely fired from a Tech9 likely modified to fully automatic mode. They remained at the scene for the four hours that it took to collect all of the evidence and remove the bodies of the dead young men.

Both Dave and Robin were glad that they would have the next three days off.

***

On their first day back, they both showed a renewed spirit and were ready for action. Dave had worked two of the days at security details. He worked a high school football game at Elder High School and a college football game at the University of Cincinnati. Robin's partner took a night off and the two drove to Nashville, Indiana for a shopping trip and spent the night at the legendary Brown County Inn.

They were patrolling downtown when they received a call to the Public Library for a male exposing himself. When they walked toward the front entrance, they saw a male fitting the description. Robin walked up to the male who immediately took a swing her, knocking her hat off. Robin kicked the man's legs out from under him and rolled him onto his back to handcuff him. A crowd started gathering surrounding the two cops and screaming obscenities. Dave got on the radio and put out an assistance call and the sirens could be heard immediately. Dave grabbed the male by the neck and pulled him up to his feet as police cars were arriving in droves. The crowd was getting more and more rowdy until a canine unit pulled and the dog was brought out from the car. The crowd thinned quickly and the prisoner was taken to jail.

As they left the Justice Center, Dave said, "It is early October and the systemwide transfer portal is open." "Are you looking to transfer back to District Five? You made it clear you did not want to be here in District One." Robin gave a thoughtful look and replied, "I gave it serious thought, but I am enjoying my time and having you as a partner. There is always the possibility that the City may transfer one or both of us. Let's enjoy what we do for as long as we can."

IV

When the two cops got into the cruiser for their shift, Robin turned on the computer and saw a call awaiting them. It sent them to 1134 Sycamore Street Apartment 3F for a domestic violence complaint. When they arrived at the address, they saw a 1900's era row house and they had to climb the three flights of stairs and then walk down a hallway to get to the apartment. Robin knocked on the door and a petite woman answered the door in disheveled clothing with fresh blood on it. Dave could see though the open door and there was a man sitting on a couch in the living room. They walked in the door and Dave told Robin to take the female to the kitchen and get her side of the story and Dave would talk to the male. Dave walked into the living room and asked the male to stand up. The male got off the couch and lunged toward Dave, grabbing his holstered gun. Dave reacted by striking the man with his palm breaking the man's jaw. The man screamed in pain and dropped to the floor. Robin came running into the room asking, "What the hell happened?" Dave answered, He grabbed my gun and I hit him in the jaw with my palm, I heard a loud crack so I believe I broke it. Call for a rescue unit and a boss." Robin pressed the transmit button and said, "1204, I need a rescue unit and a supervisor at 1134 Sycamore third floor."

They were less than two blocks from the fire house, so the paramedics and the sergeant arrived at the same time. The sergeant looked at the male, who was still on the floor screaming and asked, "What happened?" Dave looked at the sergeant and replied, "I think I want a lawyer." The sergeant looked at Robin and said, "You follow the rescue unit to the hospital and arrest him for domestic violence as soon as he is released. The city attorney will decide what additional charges to file." The sergeant looked at Dave and said, "I will drive you to Internal Investigations so they can initiate their investigation." The sergeant drove to an office building just outside of the downtown area and the two walked into an unmarked office on the first floor. The entered a waiting room with a glass partition separating the room from the interior. The sergeant walked up to the receptionist who picked up the phone to make a call. Less than one minute later, a uniformed Lieutenant walked to the interior door, opened it and motioned Dave to follow him.

He took Dave to a room with one table and three chairs. Dave immediately saw the video camera mounted on the wall and the table had three microphones attached to it. The Lieutenant said, "I understand you have invoked your right to counsel. There is a phone on the wall to your right for you to call the FOP. It is not a taped line." Dave called the FOP office and the secretary told him that the attorney would arrive in less than one hour. Dave hung up the phone and walked to a chair that the Lieutenant pointed him toward. Once seated, the Lieutenant reached into a pouch and pulled out a single sheet of paper. He looked at Dave and said, "This is a _Garrity_ Warning letter which I will read to you and ask you to sign. If you refuse to sign, you will immediately be fired. I will then ask you several questions. If you refuse to answer or provide false information, you will be immediately terminated from your employment with the city. Do you understand?" Dave nodded his head up and down and the Lieutenant read the form to Dave. Dave signed the form just as the FOP lawyer arrived at the room. The attorney opened the door and told the Lieutenant, "I would like to speak to my client and I want assurance that all recording devices are off." The Lieutenant said nothing was being recorded and walked out of the room.

Once the Lieutenant left, the attorney said, "The fact that they are invoking *Garrity* means they are not interested in a criminal prosecution. Answer all the questions truthfully and, if they move to invoke an administrative violation, we will deal with it then. I am permitted to be present for the interview, but I am not allowed to speak. If you feel uncomfortable at any point, ask to speak to me and the Lieutenant will have to leave the room and turn off all recording devices. Do you have any questions before this begins?" Dave shook his head and the attorney motioned the Lieutenant to return.

The Lieutenant threw two switches and Dave saw a green light on the camera and red lights for the microphones come on.

Q   Tell me about the run

A   We received a radio call about a domestic violence at the address

Q   What happened when you arrived?

A   A female answered the door. I saw the male sitting on a couch in the living room

Q   What was the male doing

A   Nothing, just sitting there

Q   What happened next

A   Officer Milner took the female to the kitchen. I
     approached the male and asked him to stand up.
     When he got up from the couch, he immediately
     lunged at me and grabbed my gun

Q   Was he able to get it out of the holster

A   No

Q   What happened next

A   When I felt him pull on my gun, I reacted
     instinctively and used an open palm strike hitting
     his left cheek. I heard a distinct popping sound and
     he dropped to the floor screaming in pain

Q   Will your partner tell the same story

A   My partner did not witness anything. She came
     running in when she heard the scream

The Lieutenant turned off the video and audio recording
systems. When they left the room, the FOP lawyer told
Dave, "We will deal with any administrative action if
happens.Until then, just keep yoiur head down and be
low-key. The Lieutenant told Dave, "You are hereby
notified that your police powers have been suspended. I
need you to turn over your badge and gun now. You will
report to the Telephone Crime Reporting Unit tommorrow
at eight o'clock.

Dave reported to the TCRU office at eight o'clock as ordered wearing his uniform without a badge or gunbelt. There were three people seated at desks when he entered. A sergeant pointed to a desk and told him that he would be answering the phone and obtaining information to complete police reports of crimes that did not require a police officer to be present. The sergeant told him the kinds of reports he would be expected to complete would be criminal damaging, theft from vehicles and menacing. The reports would be entered into the computer and then forwarded to the District investigator for follow-up.His shift would be eight hour days Monday thru Friday.

Dave took information for nine reports his first day. He asked the sergeant about taking his lunch and was told he could leave to pick up whatever he wanted, but was not aurhorized to operate a police vehicle. At the end of the day, he was mentally worn out from the boredom of the job, but happy that he was still getting paid. He went home and collapsed on the couch to sit and watch television telling his wife that he had lost his appetite.

Dave was halfway through his fourth day when he saw a uniforned sergeant enter the room. The sergeant walked over to Dave and handed him a letter with the heading, "Cincinnati Police Department; Office of the Chief." The letter said, "The investigation into this matter has been completed and there is no evidence that any violation of police policy or criminal law occurred. You are hereby reinstated to full duty effective immediately." The sergeant then handed Dave a brown manila envelope containing his firearm and his badge. The sergeant left the room without making any further statements. Dave immediately left the office and went to his locker to grab a holster for his weapon to wear home.

***

Dave walked into the roll call room and was immediately greeted with slaps on the back and high fives. He sat down next to Robin as the sergeant went through the roll call information for the day. There was nothing said between the two until they got into the cruiser. Robin asked, "What the hell happened partner?" Dave answered, "They put me into the penalty box pending their investigation, which was a joke. I spent four days typing telephone crime reports until a sergeant from the headhunters gave me back my badge and gun. It sucked!"

The two were patrolling downtown when they received a call to respond to Fountain Square to investigate a male subject acting suspiciously. As soon as they pulled up, people began pointing toward a man standing next to the fountain wearing military garb. The two approached and suddenly the man ran directly at them tackling Robin. Dave heard her whimper softly and saw blood coming out of her shirt. Dave punched the man in the face so hard that he dislocated two knuckles, but was able to call for help and a resuce unit. After less than thirty seconds with no paramedics, Dave forgot about his hand and scooped up Robin, placing her in the police car. He then made a kamakazi drive through downtown to get her to the hospital. When He pulled into the University of Cincinnati Medical Center Emergency Department entrance, he laid on the air horn until two doctors and a nurse came out to check on the commotion. The medical people immediately removed Robin's gunbelt, which was acting as a torniquet to slow the bleeding and now blood was spurting out of her abdomen. They threw Robin on a guerney and wheeled her directly into surgery. Dave followed and was told to wait in the surgical waiting area. Once things settled down, Dave began to feel intense pain in his hand and walked to the Emergency Department to get it looked at. The nurse placed a cold pack on his hand until the doctor could look at it. The doctor popped the two knuckles back into place causing Dave to scream in pain. The doctor told Dave that he dislocated the knuckles and to keep an ice pack on his hand. He also gave Dave a shot for pain. When Dave returned to the surgical waiting room, he found it full of police brass. The Captain from District One, two Assistant Police Chiefs and the Chief were there waiting to hear the result of the surgery.

A doctor walked into the room and told everyone that Robin had been stabbed just below her bullet proof vest and that she had lost a lot of blood. He announced that the medical team was able to stabalize her, but that she was not out of the woods. They were pumping blood into her as fast as they could, and that more would be known in the next several hours. The District One Commander told Dave to go home and that he would call Dave as soon as they had more information. He also told Dave that he would need to call for a car to pick him up at the hospital because his cruiser had been taken as evidence. The Captain told Dave that he would send detectives to Dave's house to get his statement and that the suspect was in the emergency room with a broken jaw and nose.

Dave went out to the front entrance of the hospital and called communications for a ride back to the District. Fifteen minutes later, a female cop pullled up in front to take him to his car. She said, "Damn man, you hit that son of a bitch with a snow plow? You busted his face good." The pain meds were starting to kick in and Dave asked the female to just take him to his home in District Three. The cop called the Captain to ask for permission and was told to take Dave wherever he wanted to go.

Dave walked into the house with the big bandage wrapped around his hand and his wife's face grew ashen in fear. Dave told her he was fine, but that Robin had been stabbed and was in surgery. They prayed together that God would watch over Robin and she would pull through. Dave was sleeping on the couch when the Captain called him on his cell, telling him that Robin was out of surgery and was being moved to a room. He told Dave, "The doctors are happy with her progress and expect a full recovery in a matter of weeks. Dave hung up and immediately went back to sleep.

**

He saw improvement each day. Because the injury Dave suffered was to his gun hand, Dave was unable to return to work for four weeks. He had to go through physical therapy to regain the strength in his right hand and then pass the firearm qualification before being allowed to return to duty.

When he returned to duty, Dave worked the shifts as a one person car for the next five weeks. He declined a new partner telling the bosses he would await the return of Robin, Every day, before the start of his shift, he would go to the hospital to see her. After she was released, Dave would call her daily and got continous updates from her partner, Dr. Elaine. No one was really sure whether or not Robin would ever return to work as a police officer, but Dave worked dilligently to keep her spirits high.

***

Dave had just left the District when a call came in of a vehicle wanted for federal weapons violations by Alcohol, Tobacco and Firearms agents. Dave drove to Eighth and Linn Streets and sat at the corner watching for the wanted car. He saw a car speeding toward the intersection and immediately gave chase. The chase went across Seventh Street through downtown, then south on Race Street to the Suspension Bridge, which connects Cincinnati with Covington, Kentucky. The car had two occupants, a male driver and a female passenger and went into Covington, turning east on Fourth Street and across a bridge into Newport, Kentucky, The driver went through a residential neighborhood and onto Washington Street where he lost control and crashed into tables ourside of a restaurant hiting four people who were merely eating lunch. Dave ordered the passenger and driver out of the vehicle at gunpoint through the passenger door as Newport Police arrived at the scene. Once they got the prisoners into handcuffs, Dave found out that an elderly married couple had been killed and another married couple were seriously injured in the crash.

The evening news broadcast that he had violated police policy by pursuing the car across the state line and that the couple that survived were filing suit against him and the City for their injuries suffered as a result of the crash. The suspect later pled guilty to two counts of Murder because the Commonwealth of Kentucky took the death penalty off of the table.

V

Robin woke up in a hospital bed feeling sore and weak, but had no idea how she got there. A doctor walked into the room and said, "Lady, you just went through a really difficult surgery. You are very lucky to be with us. Do you remember what happened?" Robin said, "I remember walking on Fountain Square approaching a man and him jumping on me. I don't know what happened after." The doctor said, "You were stabbed just below your ballistic vest and began bleeding heavily. Your partner picked up and put you into the police car and drove you here. You will need to get all of your strength back, and that is going to take some time." Robin asked, "Am I going to be able to return to duty?" The doctor grimaced and answered, "We will not know that for weeks, maybe months. It will depend on how you respond to rehabilitation. You will be a guest of ours for several weeks, until you regain the strength to fend for yourself. I am told your life partner is an emergency room doctor and that will help get you home faster."

Robin was taken out of the hospital in a wheelchair to a waiting car driven by Elaine. It had been twenty-six days in the intensive care unit of the hospital and Robin was going crazy at her inability to do much of anything by herself. Elaine hugged her tightly and drove her home to be in her own bed. She immediately called Dave to tell her that she was at home and that she was scheduled to start physical therapy the next day.

Robin was driven to her PT appointment by Elaine and met her therapist, a woman named Chelsea, who told Robin that they woud start slowly and increase the intensity each visit until they reached whatever level of recovery they could get to. She told Robin that it was immposible to know whether Robin would ever be able to return to police work but, as long as Robin put in the effort, Chelsea would work just as hard to get her back to full duty. Robin smiled meekly and said, "I want you to beat me up. I do not cry and I will give one hundred percent to getting my strength back. They would meet and Robin screamed in pain a lot, but never once cried. She could feel her strength returning slowly. At the end of the first month, Robin would go to the gym with Dave once a week and got back into running on a rubber-surface indoor track.

Dave called Robin and said he wanted to take her to lunch. When they ordered and the waitress left, Dave said, :I am having a problem at home. My wife is expressing concern about the amount of time I spend with you and believes we are having an affair. I was thinking that you and Elaine and my wife and I should have dinner together and you can explain that you are not into men. I need your help with this.: Robin thought for a moment and replied, "I understand her concern and think that chatting with her will clear up any issues."

The four met for dinner at a steakhouse that was once a Cincinnati Police District station. Dave was nervous as to how the evening would play out and his wife was less than thrilled as well. They ordered drinks and Robin began the discussion with, "I understand that you would have concerns about a male and female being partnered in a police car for ten hours at a time, so let me try to allay some of those fears. Your husband has absolutely nothing that interests me. We saw everything there was to see at the end of the first shift together and then went on about the business of being cops. Elaine and I have discussed one of us having a baby but, if that ever happens, it will be the result of an embryo fertilized in a tube. The male anatomy simply has nothing to offer me. I hope that addresses your concerns. That is why I brought Elaine along, so she can also answer any questions you may have."

***

With the one year anniverary of her injury approaching, Robin became concerned that she would be terminated from the police department and have to get a medical disability. She increased her physical workout regiment and, with only three weeks left, received a medical release to return to light duty. She was assigned to be a desk officer in District Five where she would answer phones, deal with walk-in complaints, and screen visitors to the Investigative Unit and Captain. She wore her police uniform with only a firearm instead of a full police belt, which reduced the weight she had to carry. After three months of light duty, the city doctor authorized her back to full duty and she returned to District One to partner with Dave.

On their first shift back together, the two received a radio run to take a theft from a vehicle report on Ninth Street near Walnut. Robin was getting the information from the victim while Dave stood nearby. The radio barked,

"Attention District One cars, 9-1-1 caller reports a police officer laying in Gano Alley between Walnut and Vine. Robin told the woman that they would be back and both officers ran full speed toward the alley. They were the first to arrive and saw a uniformed police officer laying in a pool of blood in the alley. The smell of the expulsion of the bodily fluids and no caratoid pulse indicated that the officer was dead. Cops converged on the scene in droves and Dave requested a rescue unit and a supervisor to the scene, When the paramedics arrived, Dave told them to simply verify the death of the officer and preserve the scene for homicide investigators and asked them to return to the rig and get a sheet to cover the body. When a Lieutenant walked up on the scene, Dave and Robin began checking the alley for any possible evidence. They rounded a corner and Robin found a homeless woman hiding behind a dumpster. Robin asked the woman if she saw anything and the woman replied, "I saw two white guys in their earlly twenties running down the alley and then I heard the sound of two gunshots. When I peeked around the corner, I saw the cop laying on the ground. The two men were gone." The two cops turned the witness over to a uniformed cop and began re-tracing the steps that the suspects came from. They arived at the Vine Street end of the alley and Robin turned south while Dave went north. They wanted to check the local businesses to see if the two suspects were running from a crime.

Dave looked into the window of each business he passed. When he got to a cigar store, he could not see anyone inside. He walked into the store and there were no employees to be seen. Dave walked behind the counter and into a back office where he saw a seventy year old man laying on the floor bound on his hands and legs with duct tape. His mouth was also covered with the gray tape. Dave pulled out a folding knife and cut the tape from the man's legs and hands and then ripped the tape covering his mouth causing the man to scream in pain.

The victim told Dave that the two white males came into the store and one pulled a gun on him, ordering him to open the safe in the back office. They took several hundred dollars in cash and tied him up. Dave asked for a description to put out a broadcast and the old man got a smile on his face. He told Dave that he had just installed a high resolution video surveillance system in the store and that it would have pictures of the suspects. The video clearly showed the two men and Dave put out a broadcast of the men and what they were wearing and that they were wanted for Aggravated Robbery and Kidnapping. Dave advised police communications to dispatch a forensics team and detectives to his location. Robin walked into the store moments later.

The crime scene techs arrived and Dave told them to get the pictures of the two suspects and use facial recognition to match against the inmate data base of the Hamilton County Justice Center. He assumed that this was not their first rodeo and they might well be in the system. Dave told Robin, "My guess is that the officer did not initiate the contact and had no clue they had just committed the robbery. They shot the officer out of a fear of being caught."

The facial reconition software got a hit on one of the two men. The man named Tommy Massey was a twenty-two year old white male who had just completed a six month sentence for a theft offense and showed an address two blocks away on Vine Street. The two cops walked to the apartment building and rang the buzzer of the apartment manager. The manager told them Massey lived with another male and that Massey had come home in the last hour alone. The manager said that he did not know the name of the other man living there. Dave called for a SWAT Team and asked a supervisor to get a telephonic search warrant from a judge so they could make entry into the apartment.

The S.W.A.T team used a sixteen pound battering ram to demolish the entry door to the apartment. Armed with tactical rifles, they rushed into the apartment which consisted of three rooms, all of which could be seen from the foyer of the apartment. They searched under the bed and then opened a closet door, finding Massey hiding behind a blanket on a shelf at the top of the closet. They jerked him off the shelf, causing him to splat onto the wood floor. Dave handcuffed the man who put up no resistance and said, "Listen to my words carefully, I am only going to say this once. Who was with you and where is the gun?" The young man saw the hatred in Dave's eyes and his voice quivered as he said, "I don't know where Billy is. We split up and I came home. Billy has the gun. He is the one who shot the cop."

Robin left the apartment to get their cruiser and they took the suspect to the Homicide Unit to be interrogated. They

43

babysat the young man waiting for the detectives to arrive. They were sitting in the interrogation room when the radio cracked, "1210, shots fired, shots fired! I am at Fourteenth and Vine Street. Suspect is down. I need a supervisor and the Force Investigation Team for an Officer involved shooting." Even from the inside room, the two cops could hear sirens from all directions as other cops raced to the shooting. The dead suspect was William Gainer, and he had the gun used to kill the officer.

After transporting Massey to the Justice Center, the two cops drove back to the station to go home.

***

Dave told Robin to drive so she would not get into foot pursuits as she continued to recover. They had a slow shift that was coming to an end and decided not to get into anything that would get them into overtime. The two cruised the downtown area slowly as it was already ten thirty. They were sitting at the light at Ninth and Vine when a car blew through the intersection west on Ninth almost hitting the car that had been next to them. Dave activated the overhead lights and the car pulled over immediately. Robin approached the driver's door as Dave walked up the passenger side. Dave heard Robin say, "Don't say a word and don't do anything stupid!" Robin walked around the rear of the vehicle and said, "The driver of the car worked the beat next to me when I was in District Five." Dave answered, "He is a cop?" Robin nodded her head and said, "I know him and his wife and want to drive his car home. You can follow me." Robin walked back to the driver's side of the car and said, "Move over, we are going to take you home." Dave followed as she pulled into the driveway and helped the inebriated cop to the front door. Robin handed the woman who answered the door the keys to the car as she grabbed her husband by the arm dragging him into the house. It was time to call it a night.

***

Robin had been back on full duty for a week when they were called into the Captain's office just before starting their shift. The Captain told them that they were being re-assigned to a task force formed to get guns off of the streets. They would report to District One to pick up a cruiser and then go the Federal Building to brief with Alcohol, Tobacco and Firearms agents. When the two arrived at the ATF office, they were directed to a conference room where there were six other Cincinnati cops. A Cincinnati Lieutenant told them that they would be split into two teams consisting of two uniformed cops in a marked police car and two plainclothes cops to identify people with firearms. The group was taken two floors down to Federal courtroom where they were all sworn in as Federal officers, allowing them freedom from boundaries. When they rerurned to the conference room, the Lieutenant told Dave and Robin that they would be working two center Cincinnati area projects called Winton Terrace and Findlater Gardens. He told them to do regular patrol, but focus on getting guns off the street. They would be on a private radio channel to allow them to communicate with the undercover cops. Robin was driving on Winneste Avenue when the plainclothes cops identified a male.who had a semi-automatic under his shirt. Robin pulled up even with the supect and Dave jumped out of the passenger side as the suspect took off at a run. Dave tackled the man and Robin knelt on his neck as Dave retrieved the nine millimeter handgun from his waist. They put in him in the cruiser and drove him to the ATF office where a Federal Assistant US Attorney was waiting for them. The suspect was put into a holding cell and the prosecutor and the two cops went to a Federal Judge to get a search warrant for the prisoner's home. When the Judge signed the warrant, Dave, Robin and two ATF agents went to the suspect's home to serve the warrant. No one answered the front door so they kicked it in. Dave found three more firearms under the mattress of the bed and, when he entered the serial numbers into the cruiser computer, found that all had been reported stolen.

The prisoner was brought into an interrogation room where AUSA was seated at a table, He was handcuffed to hooks attached to the table and the lawyer said, "Here is your real world. We found three additional stolen guns under your mattress when we executed a search warrant there. That makes a total of four stolen guns tied to you which is good for thirty years in prison. This is not a pansy state court where you will get concurrent sentences and be out in a year. This is Federal Court where you will do it all and the people you will be vacationing with are real badasses, not wannabees. You give us something good and three of the gun charges go away and you do maybe two years. Your choice."

The young man looked actually scared and said, "How bout I give you the gun used to kill two cops in Cincinnati about five years ago? That worth a deal?" Dave leaned down and whispered into the lawyer's ear, "I knew one of those cops and there has never been any evidence about the shooter. It was a sniper case."

The lawyer said, "You have our attention, pal. Tell us what you know and we will go from there." The prisoner said, "Killing of the cops was an initiation into the Gangster Disciples, who were trying to get a foothold in Cincinnati. The rifle was hidden in a rock wall and the shooter got it and capped the male and female cop. She was shot when she got out of the car and he was shot in the driver's seat. I can take you to where the gun is."

Robin and Dave put the suspect into their cruiser and he took them to the actual shooting site. Dave would later tell Robin that the female officer was pregnant and her husband was a former Cincinnati cop who killed himself the day after her funeral. The suspect took the officers to a rock wall and told them to remove the top layer of rocks. As Dave began removing the rocks, he saw an enclosed wooden box which turned out to be about three feet long. They removed the top cover of the box revealing a rifle wth an attached scope and a magazine of ammunition still in the weapon. Dave told Robin not to touch the gun and called for a forensic team and homicide investigators to respond to actually remove the weapon, preserving any evidence that it might contain. The crime scene techs removed the gun from the box and removed the magazine which still had three live rounds in it. The techs took the weapon back to the county crime lab and Robin and Dave took the suspect back to the ATF office. When they arrived, Dave asked whether the attorney wanted them to take the prisoner to the jail. The lawyer laughed and said, "Not an issue. I have US Marshals coming to take him to the Boone County, Kentucky jail where we have a contract to house our prisoners."

The crime lab pulled dna off the rifle which was identifed as a male currently serving a five year sentence for an unaffiliated armed robbery. Cincinnati homicide investigators drove to the prison just south of Columbus, Ohio to interview the suspect. The investigator said, "We are going to make sure you get the needle for killing two cops unless you cooperate with us. It is up to you.The twenty-six year old man told them, "I was recruited into the Gangster Disciples and told to kill those cops as an initiation into the gang. After I shot them, I put the rifle where I found it and they drove me to Chicago to be far away from the scene. I stayed about eight months, but hated it, and returned to Cincinnati after I watched gang members killed in front of me. I haven't thought about it in the last five years." The investigator asked, "Who ordered the hit and did they tell you why they wanted the cops dead?" The guy said, "They wanted to send a message to the cops that they were in charge and the cops needed to be scared. The hit was ordered by Deangelo Warren, the second in command in Cincinnati at the time. The gang could not get a foothold in Cincinnati because all the leaders got busted and went to prison. Warren is doing a double nickel at Lebanon Correctional for shooting a rival gang member in Walnut Hills." The investigator asked, "Did you know that the female cop was pregnant?" The prisoner replied, "No way, all I saw was her head in the night sight and popped the cap. After I shot her, I shot through the windshield and popped the driver."

The information was forwarded to the Hamilton County prosecutor and indictments were obtained for the shooter, the man who ordered the murders and the man who drove the shooter from the scene.

VI

Dave and Robin moved to the West End projects and focused their attention on the mothers who stood watch over their kids at play to protect them from harm. They craved information on the staus of the investigation on the killing of the two cops, but none was forthcoming. Dave called a homicide detective that he had worked with in District One, but the investigator told him that there was a muzzle on everyone actually involved. The detective told Dave that the subject was not being brought up at the daily meeting of the homicide investigators where everyone made suggestions on the progress of cases.

Dave and Robin used the lever that mothers needed to help with the removal of guns from the community and to convince the women to give the location of 'community guns.' Community guns are placed in locations that can be accessed by anyone needing a weapon. The first tip from a mother revealed a location at which they recovered a nine millimeter handgun attached to two homicides and two other shootings.

The task force continued their effort with take guns off the streets of Cincinnati with an excepitional amount of success. The Federal prosecution of individuals arrested sent a message to the community that there would be a cost for carrying and using guns and the lengthy prison sentences handed out verified that.

The Feds put a tracking device on a community gun which sent a notification every time the gun was moved, Robin and Dave were posititioned near the storage space for the weapon and would snatch up the person with it as they walked away, Since most of these individuals were prohibited from possessing a firearm due to felony convictions, they were able to charge them with felony receiving stolen property and having weapons under disabilty. Again, word spread quickly throughout the community.

The two cops were waiting at a traffic light at Central Avenue and Court Street when a male knocked on the passenger window. Robin rolled the window down and the male said, "I have information that will interest you. There is a stolen yellow Toyota parked at 1100 Linn Street and there will be two dudes getting in it in the next hour. They are also carrying a nine millimeter gun. What you do with the information is up to you."

They drove down Linn Street and saw a vehicle matching the description given. Robin entered the license plate and it showed that the car was reported stolen. Dave found a parking space where they could see the car without being seen. Dave looked at Robin and said, "Damn, I wish we had picked up coffee before we came here.: Robin just laughed and the two settled in for what could be a long stay. Almost an hour later, they saw two males approach the stolen car and open the doors. Dave put the cruiser in drive and gunned the engine to take the suspects by surprise. The driver had already gotten into the car and could not get out fast enough to run, but the other suspect took off at a full run with Robin hot on his trail. Dave called the chase in on the radio and patted his prisoner down.

When he did not find the gun, he broadcast that information out on the radio. The foot chase went through the projects but the suspect was never out of Robin's sightt. It continued for almost a quarter mile when the suspect slid his hand out of sight toward his belt and then turned towards Robin, who fired a single shot which entered the left side of his body transecting the left lung and entering the heart. The suspect was dead before he hit the ground. Robin yelled into the radio, 1204A, shots fired, suspect is down. Send a rescue unit and a supervisor to my location.

Dave pushed his handcuffed prisoner into the arms of an officer who had just arrived and ran to where Robin reported she was. When he arrived, he asked Robin, "Did you find the gun partner?" Robin shook her head indicating she had not and Dave said, "Say nothing to anyone, including me until you speak to an FOP lawyer. This is going to get ugly."

A Sergeant arrived and called for the Force Investigation Team and Homicide Unit to respond and looked at Robin and said, "You want a lawyer before you make a statement, correct officer?" Robin softly replied, "yes, sir."

The Public Information Officer arrived as the media hounds were circling the drain nearby. He walked over to a set of microhones already set up and said, "A Cincinnati Police officer pursued a seventeen year ofd African-American who was running away from a stolen car. The officer fired a single shot and the suspect was pronounced dead at the scene. That is all I can say at this point as the investigation is in a very early stage, so no further information will be provided at this ponit. The Police Chief will hold a press conference tomorrow morning with updated information. I will not be taking any questions at this time."

Robin and Dave were taken to the Homicide Unit where the FIT people were waiting. They spoke to Dave first, invoking *Garrity* and telling him he was required to answer their questions. Dave walked them through the informant's meeting and information and the Senior Investigator asked, "Did you find a gun on either of the suspects or in the car?" Dave answered, "No", but said, "All of the other information provided by the informant was verified, so it was logical to assume that there was a weapon." The next question was, "Who was the person who provided the information to you?" Dave answered, "Neither one of us got his name and we had no previous dealings with him. There is a surveillance camera at the corner of Court and Central. It should provide you with a face and verify that he was there speaking to us." Dave's interview ran almost two hours.

By the time that it was Robin's turn, the FOP attorney was present. He told the investigators that he intended to invoke the collectuve bargaining agreement seventy-two hour rule for Robin to provide a written statement and that she would not be answering any questions at this time.

The evening news lead story was that a Cincinnati cop had shot and killed a seventeen year old black male and that specific information and the identity of the officer were being withheld at this time.

Robin was in the attorney's office when the news conference started. The attorney had the television on and they watched it together. The Police Chief told the press that "Officers had received informaiton about a stolen car being parked and that two males would be getting into it. The uniformed officers staked out the car and attempted to arrest the two men when they got into the car. The driver was arrested without incident, but the other suspect ran and was chased by a female officer. She fired a single shot which was fatal to the seventeen year old man. The Homicide Unit and the Force Investigation Team are in the early stages of the investigation." A reporter asked, "What can you tell us about the female officer, Chief?" The Chief reponded, "The officer is a nine year veteran of the department and her name is Robin Milner."

With the attorney's help, Robin signed a statement of the events to be turned over to FIT. The attorney told her to make no statements to anyone without him being present and to ignore the negative media coverage which was coming because this was an unarmed black male. He told her that the Administrattive Leave was normal and she would have to be cleared by the police psychologist before being allowed to return to duty. He also told her that the FOP has a peer review committee to provide any counseling she might want and that all of the members of that committee had been involved in police shootings. The city would not be able to invoke the *Garrity Rule* on these officers because it did not occur as part of their police duties. He told her to focus on her mental health and he would handle the rest.

The media outlets were in a frenzy. There were protests in the streets from activists screaming for her to be charged with Murder. People were interviewed who threatened Robin with physical harm based only on what they had heard from the media. People were shown on the news carrying signs saying 'KILLER COPS' and 'INDICT THE BITCH' having zero understanding of the actual facts of the case,

All of the investigative information was turned over to the Hamilton County Prosecutor's Office, who took it to a Grand Jury. The Grand Jury declined to indict and there was no administrative policy violations to be found. Robin was returned to full duty after her meeting with Dr. Don, who declared her fit for duty.

***

The six month period for the task force showed incredible results. The two teams took over one hundred firearms off the streets and got long Federal sentences for gang bangers. Returning to running a beat after this experience proved to be mundane and boring for the two cops. Dave told Robin that he had decided to take the Sergeant test and that Robin should as well. Dave scored well and was placed fifth on the list while Robin failed the examination by two points, which was sad since she would have been likely promoted by simply passing the test, Cincinnati, like many other cities, set up three separate lists for promotional examinations. The first list was the top scorers, the second list was minority males and the third list was other minority participants. Every time the City promoted two from the primary list, they would promote an additional person from the other lists.This was part of a consent decree with the Federal Court resulting from a lawsuit filed by the Department of Justice.

Robin passed the Police Specialist test and got promoted. Dave took and scored well on the Sergeant's test and awaited his promotion which, sadly, would break up Batman and Robin. Robin told Dave that she was thrilled that he would become a supervisor and would probably transfer back to District Five when they were split up. Until then, they would continue to aggressively patrol the streets.

Dave and Robin were dispatched to a silent burglar alarm at a produce warehouse along the river. They parked on the side of the building and walked around checking the windows and doors. In the rear of the building Robin found a door that appeared to have been pried open with some kind of bar. Dave called communications and requested additional units as the building covered more than a full city block. He also requested a canine unit be dispatched. It took six police cars to provide a perimeter. The canine unit pulled in the back of the building and Officer Doug Hatter got out with his canine named Ajax. Hatter told the two cops to remain behind him at all times so that they would not get bitten. He said, "The dog does not understand that you have a badge and are the good guys. He only knows me." The canine was on a ten foot lead and immediately picked up a scent. Dave and Robin followed as the dog moved along the aisle between the cartons of produce stacked on both sides, After a considerable distance, Dave looked up on the top of the boxes and saw a male trying to hide. Hatter yelled, "Come down or I send the dog up to help you come down, I promise it will not end well for you." The man yelled back, "I ain't coming down, send the dog!" Hatter released the clip on the leash and announced, "Ajax, seek." The dog just sat for a few seconds and then took off at a full run. Less than one minute later, the cops heard a scream and the man fell fifteen feet onto the cement floor. Hatter walked over to the man sprawled out on the floor and said simply, "Schmuck.: Dave handcuffed the suspect and Hatter smiled and said, "You get to take him to the hospital because the jail will not accept a prisoner who has been bitten without a medical release."

The two cops drove to University Medical Center and took the handcuffed prisoner into the Emergency Room. Robin told the nurse the man had been bitten by a police canine and she led them into a treatment room. The nurse told the cops that they needed to remove the handcuffs for the doctor to treat him. Dave took the handcuffs off while Robin removed her Taser from its holder saying, "Get stupid and you get to ride the bull," which is the jail slang for someone who has had ninety thousand volts introduced into their body from the Taser. When the handcuffs were off, the nurse told the guy to drop his pants and his underwear for her to see the wound. Naked from the waist down, Robin looked and laughed saying, "Gee, I thought a burglar would have bigger balls." The nurse told the guy to get up on the treatment bed laying on his stomach so that she could disinfect the dog's teeth marks in his ass. The guy let out a yell when she applied the alcohol wipe around the wound, to which Dave commented, "What a wimp." When the wound was cleaned, the nurse told the cops, "The doctor will be in shortly to give him a shot." Moments later, the doctor came in and looked at the depth of the bite marks and gave the prisoner the shot. He told the cops that they could pick up the medical release they needed at the service desk and that the jail would now accept him. The priisoner whimpered and whined all the way to the Hamilton County Justice Center.

***

Two months later Dave was promoted and told that he would be tranfered to District Four, which serves the northern part of the City. On the final shift the two would be working together, Dave made plans to take Robin to the Phoenix restaurant, one the premier steak houses in downtown Cincinnati. He told the other cops before roll call his plans to surprise Robin and asked them to cover for him while they ate. Dave pulled up in front of the Precinct Restaurant and pressed the transmit button on the radio, advising communications that they would be out of the car. They walked toward the entrance and Robin asked, "What the hell is going on partner?" Dave smiled and said, "I wanted to make our last shift special, so dinner is on me," When they walked in the door, the woman standing at the podium asked, "Can I help you officers?" Dave smiled and answered, "We would like a table." The woman got a shocked look on her face and said simply, "Follow me." As she led the two cops to a table, the patrons in the restaurant followed their every step because uniform cops never ate there. It was an expensive place to eat.

The woman seated the two at a table in the corner of the room and asked if they would like to order drinks. Dave ordered two coffees and the woman walked away. A man in a three piece suit walked up to the table and said, "Welcome, and I hope you enjoy your meal with us. Mr. Ruby told me that your meal is on him today. I would suggest the prime rib, it is fresh and delicious." Dave smiled and replied, "I just hope we get to eat it. Thank Mr. Ruby and bring me one check for the full amount.

Just as they ordered the prime rib for each of them, communications gave them a radio run to Ninth and Main for a traffic accident. Before Dave could acknowledge he heard, "Car 1209, I will take that call. Give 1204 a disregard." Moments later the radio cracked, "Car 1204, respond to the Walnut Café for a fight in progress." Immediately Dave heard, "Car 1207, I will take that." Following that, "Car 1202, we are a two person car, also responding. Give 1204 a disregard." Communications must have gotten the memo because their number was not called again.

Dave smiled as the waiter put a bread basket on the table. He told Robin, "My wife is ecstatic that our partnership is breaking up. She still sees you as a threat." Robin laughed and answered, "I did my best to convince her that you are not my type, guess I failed." She said, "I put in for a transfer to Central Vice Unit and am awaiting an answer. Getting promoted opens a world of doors into the specialized units and I think vice might be fun." Robin continued, :Elaine has decided that she wants to get pregnant the old fashioned way. She found a doctor in the

ER who will have intercourse with her once a week for as long as it takes for her to be impregnated. He has signed an agreement waiving all of his parental rights in return for no parental responsibility. This should be interesting to watch. I hope to have a baby at some point, but it will be through invitro fertilization."

When the two got back into the cruiser, Dave waited for the first radio call to be broadcast and said, "Car 1204, give that car a disregard, we will handle the call." That told the officers working that they were done eating. The two hugged at the end of the shift and promised to stay in contact.

VII

Robin got her transfer back to District Five and Dave was assigned as a shift sergeant in District Four. When Robin walked into the roll call room at District Five, she felt like she had never left. Almost all of the same officers she had worked with were still there and there were hugs and high-fives from all. She was thrilled when the sergeant told her she would get her old beat back as well. It covered the area surrounding the campus of the University of Cincinnati.

She spent her first shift re-connecting with the business owners and residents in her beat. She wanted the rapport back that she had with them that had helped her solve cases in the past. She had just pulled out of Burnet Woods Park when the emergency tones dropped from communications. The dispatcher said, "Attention all cars all departments, we have a report of a University Police Officer shot at the entrance to U.C. Hospital. Robin activated the siren and lights and almost struck a passing car as she turned onto Martin Luther King Drive. Screaming down the road, she blew through a major intersection at almost ninety miles per hour. When she arrived at the entrance less than two minutes later, the scene was total chaos. Doctors and nurses ran out of the building and were treating the officer on the sidewalk. A bullet grazed his neck and nicked his caratoid artery, but he was still alert and conscious. Robin ran over to the officer and pulled his body worn camera off of his chest, taking it into the hospital police office where she could view it. The camera clearly recorded the shooting and the suspect. Robin put out a description over the air and then placed the camera in an evidence envelope from the office. When she went back outside, she saw a homicide detective and gave him the envelope with she had signed and dated to keep the chain of custody for the evidence.

Robin went back to her cruiser and started looking for the suspect. She knew the area well and had ideas as to where the suspect would run. She was in a parking lot checking behind a set of dumpsters when she heard an officer scream into the radio that he suspect was running behind a neighboring hospital and had fired shots at the officer. Robin ran a short distance to the other side of that hospital just as the suspect came around a corner. She ordered him to drop his gun just as he fired a shot at her. She fired two shots, both of which hit the suspect in the chest, killing him instantly. She got on the radio and requested a supervisor, homicide and a rescue unit for an officer involved shooting. Moments later, Robin was shocked that the first supervisor to arrive was Dave. Dave looked at her and said, "Say nothing to anyone about what happened. Tell whoever that you want an FOP attorney present." Within minutes the area was swarming with cops and supervisors. Robin told a Lieutenant that she wanted a lawyer and the Lieutenant directed Dave to drive Robin to the homicide office and told another supervisor to call the FOP office for her.

Dave drove slowly to the downtown Homicide Office so that Robin would have the opportunity to get her wits back. He told her, "When you talk to the homicide dicks, tell them you will only make your statement once, so they can talk to you or wait until the Force Investigation Team arrives. I was involved in a shooting my second year on the job and it turned into a nightmare. When you make multiple statements, they match what you said in each looking for inconsistencies. Doesn't mean you lie, just that you remember something in the second statement or forget something in the first. And do not say a word until the FOP lawyer is there with you. I will stay with you, but they will not let me into the interrogation room. You will get a few days off until you sit down with Dr. Don, who is a really good guy and not there to screw you over. He will only gig you if he thinks you are a threat to yourself. Whatever happens, do not beat yourself up over this. The bad guy made the decision that cost him his life. Afterwards, I will drive you home. You can get your car later.".

***

On her next shift, Robin was driving the area where most of the off-campus housing was when she saw flames coming from the roof of an apartment building. She called for the fire department and ran into the building and up to the thrid floor. She knocked on all the doors yelling, "FIRE, GET OUT!" She reached apartment 307 and banged on the door with no response.She banged again and was getting ready to move on when a woman walking by said, "The woman who lives in that apartment is in her eighties and is home. I saw her enter about thirty minutes ago." Robin grabbed a fifteen pound fire extinguisher and pounded the door handle with all her strength.

She was exhausted when her seventh strike cracked the frame of the door and it opened. Robin walked into the smoky apartment and was searching when her foot hit somethng. She got on her knees and felt the limp body of the woman, Locking her hands under the woman's arms and began dragging the two hundred and sixty pound woman toward the exterior door. Each pull was only moving the victim inches, but Robin would get a breath and then pull again. She was becoming dizzy and feeling like she would vomit when she heard a male voice yell, "FIRE DEPARTMENT, ANYONE UP HERE?" With her last bit of strength Robin yelled, 'CINCINNATI POLICE, DOWN HERE!" Three firemen entered the room and scooped up the woman, getting her out of the apartment. A fourth fireman grabbed Robin by the arm and helped her back into the hallway and then out of the building, placing her on a step in the rear of the paramedic rig. A paramedic put an oxygen mask on her face and opened the valve to push one hundred percent oxygen into her lungs.She began coughing and spitting up the remnants of the smoke that was deep in her lungs. After a few minutes, she began to be able to breathe without the assistance of the oxygen. A Lieutenant walked up and told her to go to the hospital, but she told him she was fine. He looked at Robin and said, :That was not a request, it was an order." The Lieutenant looked at a uniformed police officer and said, "Take her to the hospital, NOW!" Robin received a breathing treatment in the Emergency Room and began to regain her strength. When the treatment was done, Robin asked the nurse to check on a large woman brought in from a fire on Wheeler Street. The nurse left the room and returned shortly after saying, "She is alive and they are working on her now. She suffered a stroke and will have a long recovery, but she is alive thanks to whoever got her out."

The Emergency Room doctor told her to take a couple of days off and gave her a medical order to be given to the Police Department. He prescribed an inhaler to help cleanse her lungs of the gunk she had ingested.

***

Dave walked into his first roll call and told the officers. "I may be new, but I have no need to impress anyone. As long as you serve the people of Cincinnat, we will get along. I am not pushy and will not tolerate anyone on a power trip." Dave was given the task of approving the reports from the previous day. The Lieutenant handed him a red pen and told him to mark gramatical errors or missing parts of the reports and return them to the officers to fix them. Dave only looked for glaring errors and ended up sending five back to officers to be re-done.

Dave decided to drive around because his eyes hurt from reading over a hundred crime reports. He heard a radio call from an officer to have a boss respond to his location. Dave took the call and arrived at the house ten minutes later. The officer told him that an eighty-two year old man was found in the house dead by his daughter and that no foul play was indicated as the man was under the care of hospice and had serious medical issues. Dave had received training at the academy for First Line Supervisors that a supervisor was required to respond to all dead body calls and to notifiy the coroner's office of the manner of death so they could decide whether to release the body to a funeral home or have it transported to the coroner for an autopsy. Dave called the coroner and the person who answered Dave knew from when the guy worked in homicide before he retired. The investigator told him to release the body to the funeral home.

Dave decided to take a slow ride to the area surrounding Xavier University, He was on Victory Parkway when a broadcast came out for a white male wanted for an Arson. Dave saw a male walking up Victory Parkway who matched the description. He crossed into the oncoming lane and pulled up next to the walking man. Dave said, "Mind if we talk for a minute?," but got no answer. Dave stayed even with the man and repeated, "You need to stop so we can talk." The man broke into a full run and Dave followed in the cruiser. When he got even with the suspect, Dave opened the driver's door of the cruiser hitting the man in the back and sending him end over end down rhw sidewalk. Each bounce on the cement sidewalk shredded clothing and ripped away skin. When the man came to a stop he was whimpering and bleeding. Dave called for a rescue unit and a Lieutenant to respond. The dispatcher replied that a rescue unit was en route, but there were no Lieutenants available in District Four. The radio cracked with, "Car 400, show me responding. 400 is the unit number assigned to the Captain who commands the District. Before Dave could transmit he heard, "Car 11, I am two blocks away, show me also responding. Car 11 is assigned to an Assistant Police Chief.

The Assistant Chief pulled up in his unmarked car and looked at Dave saying, "Tell me a story." Dave explained what had transpired and the Assistant Chief pushed the transmit button saying, "Car 11, contact traffic section and tell them I want the Major Accident Investigation Team to respond to this location. The paramedic unit and the Captain arrived at the same time. The medics performed a cursory look at the susect's injuries and said, "He needs to go to the hospital, but you cannot put handcuffs on due to his injuries. A police officer will need to ride with him. The Captain got on the radio and requested a two person car to come to the location. When they arrived, the Captain said, "One of you needs to ride with the prisoner and the other follow." The Assistant Chief looked at Dave and said, "You need to hope that this is the right bad guy. Your career depends on it."

VIII

Robin put in an application to join the Central Vice Unit and was interviewed by the female Lieutenant Commander at their office. The Lieutenant wanted to know why Robin wanted to join the unit. Robin answered, "I like being where the action is boss. I was part of the Batman and Robin team and we were active and aggressive in District One." The Lieutenant got up from her chair and shook Robin's hand saying, "Report here at eight o'clock Monday morning, welcome to the team."

Robin spent the first week in Vice meeting the other members and getting familiar with how they do business. The last day of the week she was told that she would be doing a reverse prostitution sting on Monday. She would be a hooker and arresting the 'Johns' wanting to pay for sex. She was told that she needed to get the man to say the sex act and the amount to be paid in order for the case to hold up in court.

Robin walked into the office wearing a white mesh blouse with no bra and a short skirt. She did not tell anyone she never wears underwear. She found a pair of high heel shoes and literally looked the part. Her three man team dropped her off a block from where she would be and she walked up the street to the corner. She was there about forty-five minutes when a car stopped with a man who appeared to be in his early sixties. The man told Robin he was in between meetings and wanted oral sex from her. He told Robin he was willing to pay one hundred dollars for her service. Robin told the man to pull down the street and turn right into the alley and turn off his ignition and she would take care of his needs. The man smiled and followed the directions. When he turned the ignition off, three cops walked up and arrested him. Two took the man to an unmarked car while the third drove his car to the vice office.

A second three man team arrived moments later and Robin went back to smiling at the passing cars. A new Cadillac Escalade pulled up and stopped. The driver, a large black male, rolled the passenger window down and said, "You are working my corner, bitch. Take your ass somewhere else." Robin looked into the window and replied, "I must have missed the sign that this is your corner. Truck on down the road, pal. You can have the street back when I am done here." The driver said, "Tell you what. How about you let me slide my nine inches into you ass and I get to hear you whimper as it goes in. When I shoot my load, you get two hundred dollars." Robin smiled and said, "Let's see the cash big spender." The man reached into his pocket and brought out a roll of bills, thumbing through the money showing multiple one hundred dollar bills,

Robin gave the man the same directions she had given the previous John. The man got a scowl on his face and said, "Get in the car bitch and let's get this done?" The smile went away from Robin's face and she said, "This ain't negotiable. You want to do this, you play by my rules." The man reached to the center console and removed a porn magazine showing a silver plated .45 caliber semi-automatic handgun. He tapped the gun and said,. "I said get in the car bitch." Robin looked at the weapon and replied, "My three pimps are not going to like you threatening me with a gun. I suggest you turn and look out the driver's window." The man looked out the window and saw a large male wearing a badge on a lanyard pointing a gun at him. He then looked forward through the winshield and saw another man pointing a gun at him. He then looked in the rear view mirror and saw the third officer pointing a weapon at him. Robin reached into the car and picked up the .45. Smiling she said, "And, by the way, you are under arrest." They brought the man out of the car and placed him in handcuffs. He said, "You are a goddamn cop, bitch." Robin smiled and said, "First intelligent thing you have said. Love the car, we will love driving iit." A search of the interior of the car revealed a zip lock bag with glassine envelopes containing a cream color subtance believed to be crack cocaine.

Robin rode in the passenger side of the front seat while the second vice cop rode in the back with the prisoner. Because of the amount of paperwork this arrest would generate, the sting was done for the day. When they arrived at the vice office, Robin entered the prisoner's information into the police computer and came up with a warrant for him out of Texas for felony assault in Houston. Robin walked into the interrogation room and said, "Damn shame we don't get to keep you, Houston Police want you worse than we do. You will love your new home in Huntsville. They have a cell with your name on it."

Robin reported for her shift and the Commander motioned her into the office. She told Robin that the Unit had received a report that a male was recruiting hookers to work the downtown hotels and was using force and intimidation to get women into his stable of women. Robin was to sit in the bar at the Westin Hotel and see if she could get the pimp to make contact. She would have two cops in the bar to cover her. She was to ignore any solicitations as they were there for the specific purpose of trapping the pimp.

Robin dressed the part wearing her short skirt and white blouse with no bra. She sat at a table and ordered a coctail which sat in front of her untouched. She could see other women seated at tables and smiling at the males who came into the bar. A male in a business suit walked up to the table and asked Robin if he could buy her a drink. She smiled and declined saying, "Sorry pal, I am waiting on someone special." The man walked to another table and sat down next to another woman.

After a little more than an hour of sitting and nursing her drink, a man came up and pulled out a chair at her table. When he sat down, Robin smiled and said, "Shag your ass out of the chair, I am waiting on someone." The man took off his jacket showing his muscular build and said, "This hotel is reserved for women who work for my boss. You need to go elsewhere. Being here can be harmful to your well being." The look on Robin's face said it all. She looked into the man's eyes and answered, "Your boss needs to send his muscled ape to pass along a message? Tell him I have no interest in being in his stable. I am doing fine

71

without him. Now, you need to slowly get out of the chair and walk away as there is a gun pointed directly at your manhood which will ruin your miserable sex life. You need to do it now." The man sat frozen for a moment and then pushed the chair back and walked away. One of the cops protecting her got up and followed the man out the door. The other cop stayed in his seat nursing the beer he had ordered.

The male walked out to a bank of pay phones in the lobby, putting coins in the phone and making a call. When the call was over, the man walked toward the front entrance while the cop walked to the phone and wrote down the number on it to get a warrant to identify to whom the call was made. The cop then returned to the bar and sat back down. After about fifteen minutes, Robin signaled the other cops that she was calling it a night.

Robin walked into the parking lot to go to her car when the ape re-appeared. He looked at her and said, "You won't have time to reach the gun this time, bitch." Robin drove three fingers into his sternum causing him to grunt and drop to the ground. She then turned and walked away while her backup team was on top of the ape handcuffing him. The next night she was back at her table with two different vice cops there to cover her. She wasn't there long when a man in his early fifties walked up to the table and said, "We need to talk." He sat down and said, "I had to get my guy out of jail this morning, are you a cop?" Robin laughed and said, "Last I saw of your ape wannabe was when I dropped his ass in the parking lot, I walked away and never looked back, so I don't know or care what happened to him after. Now, you are cutting into my work time, so buzz off."

The man got a scowl on his face and said, "Look bitch, I control the sex trade in the hotel bars, so if you want to work here, you will do it for me. I have people from the Vice Unit on my payroll who will make your existence miserable if you do not want to play ball." Robin shot a glance at the pimp and said, "Roll with your best shot grandpa, meanwhile get out of my face." The man got up and walked away, not knowing that her team had gotten photos of his face to run facial recognition.

The third night, Robin was seated at the table when a young woman approached her and asked to sit down for a minute. She told Robin, "My boss wanted me to chat with you about getting the most out of your work here. He said to tell you that he appreciates an Alpha female and can make you a very rich woman. He has clients who like to be dominated by a woman, and they pay very well. He will offer you protection from anything you don't want to happen and no money changes hands to get you busted." Robin answered, "Okay, now you have my interest. How will this work?" The woman replied, "My boss sets up a meet here and gets you a room in the hotel to service the customer. It might involve you spanking or humiliating the John, or handcuffing him and using a dildo to open his rear end. Some men who hold executive positions want a release from having to make decisions and love to be made to beg. Think about it and we will meet here tomorrow."

Robin returned to the office and set up a meeting on how to proceed with the investigation. The Commander had a problem with a room being made available by the pimp because the team would not be able to put microphones and video in it to protect her. They also needed to establish the rules of how she operated.

It was decided that Robin would get her own room and sit in the bar for any meetings. Her backup team would be in an adjoining room with audio and video in her room.

Robin sat in the bar and this time the pimp showed up. He asked whether Robin had made a decision and she said she liked the idea, but would get her own room in the hotel. The pimp replied, "That is not the way it is done, princess." Robin grinned and replied, "I guess we have no deal then." The pimp said, "When you get arrested, maybe you will change your mind."

When he left, Robin went to the bathroom and called the Vice Unit to have one of the male cops come over and proposition her. They would leave together and that would get back to the pimp. A few minutes later, she was approached at her table and the two left together moments later. Robin could see that she was being watched by a few of the women.

The next night she was sitting quietly when a man approached her and told her that he was a police officer investigating prostitution complaints. Robin asked for a badge and the man reached into his pocket and showed a badge which she was unable to read. She asked him if she was under arrest and he told her that she was. She got up and walked out of the hotel with the man who had a bulge under his jacket which could be a gun. When the two arrived at his car, her backup team tackled the male and removed a gun from his belt. They quietly removed him and took him to the vice office where Robin was waiting for him in an interrogation room.

Robin said, "Gee moron, your badge looks nothing like mine. We now can add aggravated kidnapping to the felony impersonating a police officer, and carrying a concealed firearm and get you a nice long prison sentence. Unless, of course, you would like to cooperate with us." The prisoner looked seriously scared and told them he was paid by a man he knew as Dennis Bergan to intimidate her. That was the same name as the phone number called by the muscle ape and was enough to get a search and arrest warrant for Bergan's home and a team was assigned to stake out the residence until Bergan was at home.

A SWAT team hit the door at four in the morning, scaring the hell out of his wife and children. In the basement, the search revealed video tapes of women having sex in hotel rooms. He was removed in handcuffs and charged with mulitple felonies. When Robin walked into the interrogation room Bergan said, "I knew you were a cop. I wish I had followed my intuition."

IX

Dave was sitting in the supervisor office working on reports when an officer involved shooting at 7300 Vine Street came out over the radio. Dave ran out of the station and advised communications that he was respoding. He also told communications to notify the Force Investigation Team and the Homicide Unit to respond. When he arrived, he saw a male laying dead in the street. An officer ran over to him and told him that the officer who fired the shots was not a Cincinnati cop. There was an Elmwood Place police car parked nearby.

While he was waiting for the FIT to arrive, an unmarked black Ford Crown Victoria with blue and red lights in the grill pulled up. A man in a business suit got out of the car and walked up to Dave saying, "Are you in charge here Sergeant?" Dave nodded his head in the affirmative to which the man said, "I am the Police Chief of Elmwood Place and we will be taking over the investigation." Dave answered, "With all due respect, we have two problems. One, you are not my Chief and I do not work for you. Two, the shooting took place in the City of Cincinnati, so it is our investigation. If you choose to conduct your own investigation, that is up to you, but I am warning you not to interfere with our investigation."

Dave walked over to the young cop involved in the shooting with the Elmwood Chief at his heels. He said, "Officer, you have rights and I suggest you use them. This is a Cincinnati Police criminal investigation and our results will be turned over to the Hamilton County Prosecutor. We will be taking you to our Criminal Investgation Section to be interviewed and I need your weapon as evidence." The young cop looked to his Chief for guidance, but got none. The officer slowing withdrew his gun from its holster and handed it to Dave. Dave said, "You might seriously consider contacting the FOP to have a lawyer meet you at C.I.S.

When the FIT people arrived, Dave walked over and told them, "You cannot order him to make any statement because the *Garrity Rule* does not apply since he is not a Cincinnati cop. Give him the respect that you would give our cops and don't question him since he requested an attorney.

Dave and the Chief watched as the investigation progressed. A cop walked over and said, "Boss, I need to talk to you." Dave smiled and replied, "This is the Police Chief of Elmwood Place, anything you have to say to me can be said in front of him." The cop said, "FIT found a gun under the suspect's car. They photographed it, but did not remove it so that the forensic team can bag and tag it. They will need to remove it before the vehicle is towed. It appears that this is a good shoot."

***

Robin passed the Sergeant's examination and scored first in the secondary list which got her immediately promoted. She was assigned to first shift in District One which matched her work schedule with her partner Elaine. When she arrived for her first shift, she was given a welcome, which is unusual with newly appointed supervisors, because the older cops remembered her from her days as part of the 'Batman and Robin' team. The older cops also told the young studs that Robin was a cop's cop and to cut her some slack.

Robin was assigned to a veteran Sergeant who only had three months left until he maxed out his pension time and would be retiring. Dwane Ellis was completing his thirty-third year as a Cincinnati cop and was simply putting his time in until his retirement. Robin was happy because of the experience he could share with her during her week of mentoring time. Ellis told Robin that the key to being effective is to create a rapport with the cops, without compromising her responsibilies as a supervisor. He showed her how to approve written reports of offenses and how to return incomplete reports.

She spent the first three weeks meeting with all of the cops on her shift one-on-one to explain that her stripes were not a power trip and, if they were in the right, she would go to the mat with them. They appeared to believe that she was genuine.

Robin was sitting in a parking lot chatting with another female cop when she was dispatched to meet a car who had requested a supervisor on the entrance ramp to Interstate 75 from Sixth Street. As she sat at the traffic light at Sixth and Central, she could see the police unit with its overhead lights on behind a Dodge Charger. She pulled in behind the cruiser and activated her overhead lights.

She was seated in the car and the officer approached the driver's side. Robin rolled the window down and the officer said, "Boss, I have a situation that I have no clue how to handle. I stopped this car for running the red light and when I walked up to the car, the driver dropped a badge that says POLICE CHIEF!" He refused to submit to field sobriety tests and refuses to get out of the car unless he is told he is under arrest." Robin got out of her cruiser, grabbing her white hat and putting it on her head. She walked up to the driver's side of the Charger and knocked on the window which was rolled all the way up. The window came down a few inches and Robin said, "I am Sergeant Milner and I understand that you are a Chief of Police. Is that correct?" The male driver nodded his head up and down to indicate that the information was correct. Robin continued, "We try to extend every possible courtesy to other law enforcement professionals, but your refusal to get out of the car makes that very difficult. Would you please exit the vehicle?" The man, who appeared to be in his fifties replied, "Am I under arrest?" Robin answered. "Yes sir, you are." She then opened the driver's door and the man got out of the car. Robin said, "As you are a Police Chief, I assume you are carrying a gun." The man said, "In a holster on my right side." Robin reached around and removed a Glock 9mm from the holster. She told the officer to handcuff the prisoner and asked, "Is this vehicle owned by the Police Department, sir?" The man said it was not and Robin continued, "I would normally have another officer drive your car back to the District so you can avoid towing costs, but your lack of cooperation negates any courtesies."

She told the cop to take the prisoner back to the District and attempt to administer a breath alcohol test. She told him, "If he refuses, which I expect he will, cite him for the traffic light and the D.U.I. and then contact his police department to come and pick him up. I will sit on the car until the wrecker arrives."

After the wrecker left with the car, Robin drove back to the District. The prisoner was sitting in the sipervisor office waiting to be picked up. Robin told him, "Your vehicle was towed to our Impound Lot and you will be able to pick it up tomorrow. That is so you don't order your officer to take you to get it now." About thirty minutes later, a marked police car came and picked up their Chief. Robin handed the officer the Chief's weapon and they left.

***

Robin received a memo that she was being tranferred back to District Five on second shift. She was surprised to see it as the police department rarely puts people back in they were immediately before being promoted.

***

Robin was sitting at a desk in the supervior office when she heard, "5207, I have a vehicle refusing to srop northbound on Winton Road from the 4400 block." Robin pushed the transmit button on her radio and said, "5221, have 5207 advise speed and what the vehicle is wanted for." She heard, "5207, vehicle is at just over ninety miles per hour and is wanted for traffic violations." Robin answered, "Advise 5207 to terminate the pursuit as it is too dangerous." She heard. "5207, breaking off."

Moments later she heard, "5207 emergency traffic. I need Springfield Township Police, fire and EMS to respond to a crash at Winton and Galbraith. Vehicle I was following ran the light and hit a car broadside." Both drivers were killed by the high speed impact. Three days later, the husband of the innocent woman struck filed a lawsuit naming the officer, Robin, the Chief of Police and the City of Cincinnati alleging wrongful death.

Robin received notification that she needed to go to the office of the plaintiff's attorney for a sworn deposition. When she arrived, the City's attorney was already there and the two entered a conference room where the husband, his attorney and a court stenographer were waiting. She was administered an oath and the questioning began. The attorney asked, "Sergeant, tell us about the events leading up to the crash?" Robin explained the radio traffic and the attorney followed up with, "Where were you when this all took place and do you know if the officer actually terminated the pursuit, Sergeant?" Robin answered, "Counsellor, I was seated at a desk in the supervisor office at District Five police station, so I have no personal knowledge of what the officer did or did not do. However, I can testify that when the officer broadcast the call for medical assistance, there was no sound of a siren in the background. Ohio law requires that both the overhead lights and the siren be activated in order for a public safety vehicle to legally violate the traffic laws."

Five days later Robin received a call saying that the Judge dismmised the lawsuit stating that there was no evidence that the City had, in any manner, caused the crash.

***

Dave was out in his patrol vehicle when a call came in of a bank robbery in progress. When Dave arrived at the scene, the bank was already surrounded by officers. An officer approached and told him that the suspects had barricaded themselves in the bank and had multiple hostages. He was also told that the SWAT team was en route and their arrival time was approximately twenty minutes.

Dave used his cell phone to call the bank and a male answered. Dave asked what it would take to resolve this situation. The male demanded an armored car be backed up to the front door of the bank or he would begin killing the hostages.

Dave called Communications Section and told them to have the SWAT team bring the spare Bearcat armored vehicle with them. The SWAT team arrived with both vehicles and Dave made a call to the city highway department to come and drain all of the gas from the second armored car. He then had them put one gallon of gas into the vehicle and told the SWAT team to comply with the request and back the vehicle up to the front entrance of the bank and then open the rear door of the Bearcat before vacating it.

Dave then called the bank and told the male that the vehicle he requested was being placed as he demanded, but that all deals were off if he brought out more than one hostage to take with him. After a heated discussion, the male agreed. Three men and the female hostage exited the bank door and quicky entered the Bearcat locking the door behind them.

The Hamilton County Sheriff's heliocopter was overhead and Dave ordered all officers to back off. The SWAT member had left the Bearcat running, so the one gallon of fuel was quickly dissipating. A male got behind the wheel of the armored car and was able to drive it about two blocks before it ran out of gas.

It was now parked in the middle of the street as the driver attempted to re-start it. Using a bullhorn, Dave tried to talk the three men out of the vehicle. The male who had been the spokesperson threatened to kill the female hostage, but Dave was able to convince him that he would lose the only thing that was keeping the three males alive. The standoff continued for over three hours and the interior of the armored vehicle was becoming unbearably hot since the air conditioning was not working.

Suddenly, the rear door flew open and the female hostage exited the Bearcar. She was immediately scooped up by SWAT. One at a time, the three men came out the back door with their hands in the air and were taken into custody. The incident had resolved peacefully. Dave called the SWAT commander and thanked him for a job well done.

***

Dave scored first on the Lieutenant's examination and was immediately promoted. At the swearing-in, the Police

Chief told him to report to his office for his assignment. When he walked into the office, the secretary extended her arm to point him toward a conference room. Dave walked into the room and saw the Chief and all of the Assistant Chiefs seated at one end of the table. The Chief pointed to a chair at the other end and Dave sat down.

The Chief opened the meeting with, "I guess you are wondering why you are here? Earlier today I transferred everyone working in the Internal Investigation Section. I want you to take it over and run it. You will hand pick the people you want in it and have total freedom to operate the unit. You will report directly to me, which is why all of the Assistant Chiefs are here. I wanted them to hear that directly from me. I am giving you a blank check to make the unit as good as it can be. It is not that we have a bad police department, because this is as good an agency as anywhere in the country. But I want us to be better. You will write the policy for the operation, and decide what investigations you want to conduct."

"You have ninety days to staff the unit and then ninety days to get into full operation. Any cases through that period will be routed to the Criminal Investigation Section and the Force Investigation Team. Do you have any questions for me? If not, report to your new office and get started. Members of the unit will be prohibited from holding office or partipating in Fraternal Order of Police events. All sworn personnel will hold the rank of Sergeant to allow them to invoke *Garrity* when applicable. You will provide a detailed monthly report of the actions of the unit directly to me. Do you have any questions for me Lieutenant?"

Dave left the Chief's office and went to the office building just outside of the downtown area where the headquarters of the Internal Investigation Section was located.

When he walked into the office, he saw a secretary seated behind a plexiglass window. He introduced himself as the new commander and was buzzed into the office. There were two civilian employees seated at desks giving him strange looks as he was still in uniform.

The secretary showed him to his new office and he sat at the desk for a moment trying to take it all in. He called the two civilian employees into the office to learn what it is that they do and what, if anything, they were working on. Both of the employees were male and young. The first introduced himself as Wilbur Childs and told Dave that he was an audio/visual specialist. The other introduced himself as Henry Wilson and his specialty was behavioral analysis. They had both been told that they would not have any duties until the new commander was in place and awaited his direction.

When Dave arrived for his first full day as Commander, he wore a suit and tie to work. He immediately began drafting his requests to the Chief in an electronic mail. It said:

Chief, these are the first items I will be implementing for the new unit.

(1) NAME CHANGE...I recommend changing the name of the unit to Office of Professional Conduct and Standards. This will reflect the fact that this department demands professionalism and integrity in its personnel.

(2) FIRST EMPLOYEE...I would ask that Sgt. Robin Milner (D1) be immediately transferred to this unit. I worked with Sgt. Milner in District One when we were both street cops. Her integrity and decisiveness have never been questioned.

(3) F.I,T. I request that the Force Investigative Team be directly assigned to this unit as our investigations of police use of force are intertwined and should be on the same page.

(4) JUDICIAL OFFICER...It is my recommendation that an outside attorney, with experience as a Magistrate, be hired to conduct disciplinary hearings involving Cincinnati Police officers. This would remove the politics of having a Captain oversee violations and make recommendations of punishment in administrative cases as well as protect the rights of officers to a fair and impartial hearing. The attorney would receive compensation in the amount of one hundred dollars per hour and would only be employed on a part-time as needed basis.

(5) Request a department wide announcement of seven vacancies open to Sergeants. Have them contact the OPSC office to make an appointment for an interview.

(6) All members of this unit will sign a Non-Disclosure Agreement due to the sensitive nature of the investigations being conducted. Violation will result in immediate termination of employment and will also have a waiver of appeal rights.

Dave sent the e-mail and was shocked when he received a reply the next day. It said, "All but one of your issues have been implemented. The City Manager declined the request to appoint an outside attorney as a hearing officer, however an attorney who represents the City in all union negotiations will be available to serve as a hearing officer in any case against an officer. Sgt. Milner will report to you on Monday morning. Keep up the good work."

X

When Dave arrived at the office on Monday morning, Robin and the four team members of F.I.T were already there. Dave welcomed them and showed Robin to her new desk. He then met with all of the FIT team in the conference room telling them that they could take the day off as they would be leaving tomorrow for an intense three day force investigation training program at the FBI Academy on the Marine base at Quantico, Virginia. They all watched the nine minute video that Dave had made identifying the goals of the new unit which would be seen by all of the cops in the next several weeks.

Dave had all five sign the NDA that he had created, telling them that it was necessary for their functions needed to remain secret.

Dave met with Robin in his office telling her that she needed to begin by checking the status of investigations that were left open by the mass transfers of the former staff. She would then choose the cases which need further investigation and which to just close. He told Robin that the new unit would make a difference. He told her that the two civilian employees would be made available to her to get through the stack of files.

Robin and the two civilian employees took over the conference room after they got the list of open cases from the database. There were a total of seventy-eight cases that had not yet been resolved when the personnel were all transferred. The three started three piles for the cases as they went through them. They were:

CLOSED CASES – cases which had no futher need of investigation or ones that had been proven unfounded.

INACTIVE – cases that required further investigation.

ACTIVE – cases which required immediate action and investigation.

When they were done, the piles had twenty-two Closed, thirty Inactive, and twenty-six active cases.

The two civilians left to update the database and Robin took the Active cases and placed them on her desk for the next day.

***

When she arrived at the office the next morning, Robin grabbed the folder on top of the stack. It was a complaint from the Chief's office regarding a Lieutenant attending a press conference for the National Rifle Association where the organization publicly denounced efforts on gun control. The Lieutenant was wearing his police uniform on the stage. When interviewed, the Lieutenant claimed that he was only exercising his First Amendment right of free speech and that there was no violation. There was photographic and video evidence that he was in full uniform on the stage.

Robin walked into Dave's office and laid the file in front of him. She told him, "I am not sure what to do with this. I agree with the Lieutenant that he has a First Amendment right to free speech and I recommend we close this case. Dave looked at the information in the file and said, "I disagree. Yes, the Lieutenant does have the right to speak as an individual, but he does not have the right to speak for the police department. The wearing of his police uniform tacitly tells the public that the police department agrees with his views and that is not protected free speech. Send this case to the hearing officer with a recommendation that this officer be terminated. If the hearing officer modifies or ignores the recommendation, I have no issue with that.

Robin grabbed the file and threw it into the out basket for delivery to the hearing officer.

***

The next case on the file was a complaint from a prisoner that an officer used excessive force. Robin checked the name against the Justice Center inmates and found that the man was in jail on an unrelated charge. She drove to the Justice Center and had the man brought to an interview room. The man told her that he had been arrested for shoplifting and broke away when the officer tried to handcuff him. A foot pursuit ensued and the man was tackled by another officer and handcuffed. When the arresting officer arrived, he walked up and said, "Nobody runs from me bitch" and struck the prisoner on the right side of his face with the back of his hand. Robin asked if there

90

were any other cops present and the man told her that three other cops were there.

Robin left the interview room and went to the booking area of the jail to get the photo taken when the prisoner was brought into the facility. The photo showed swelling on the right side of his face and what appeared to be indentations that looked like human knuckles.

Robin returned to the office and contacted Police Communications Section to identify the officers present at the arrest and then ordered the three officers to come to the office with a union rep or legal counsel.

She met with each individually and placed a form in front of each to sign. Called a *Garrity Warning*, it ordered them to truthfully answer any and all questions or be terminated from their employment immediately. Each of the officers confirmed the statement that the prisoner made.

Robin ordered the arresting officer to come to the office and suggested he bring an attorney with him. When the officer and the FOP attorney arrived, the officer asked if he would be signing a *Garrity Waiver*. Robin said, "No, this is a criminal investigation and that waiver would preclude us from filing criminal charges.

Robin handed the attorney the statements of the ofher three cops and said, "I think you and your client need to discuss this before we proceed." She turned off the audio and video and walked out of the room, waiting outside until the attorney came and got her. She immediately activated the recording equipment. The attorney asked, "What specifically are you looking for?" Robin answered, "Out of deference to the eight years of service to the police department, I want to give him the opportunity to immediately resign. Otherwise, I intend to present this case to a Grand Jury and indict him." I will give you time to make a decision. She disengaged the recording devices and left the room.

When they motioned her to return to the room, the officer's badge, identification and weapon were laying on the table. The lawyer and the now former cop got up and left.

***

Dave went about staffing the new unit. He received fourteen calls for interviews and set up times for each. The first interview was a Sergeant with eighteen years on the job and was one of the ones that was tranferred out of the old group. Sergeant Ken Wills was a bit surprised when Dave handed him the NDA to sign, but reached into his pocket for a pen and signed the form immediately. Dave had looked at Wills' previous cases in the former unit and was impressed by the thoroughness of the investigations and told him that he would be receiving his transfer shortly. He welcomed him into the new unit.

Dave was able to fill the other six slots in the next three weeks and the unit was now ready to get to work. Dave received rave reviews on the video which had now been seen by over ninety percent of the sworn officers.

***

Dave's first official report to the Chief was twenty-seven pages long. It detailed the clearing of the active cases of the previous unit and the cases referred to the hearing officer for disposition. It also detailed future plans which included doing integrity checks where a person would call police and tell the officer that they had found an envelope containing cash and then see if the officer signed it into evidence.

The response from the Chief was to keep up the good work and that he was happy with the progress so far.

XI

Dave recruited college students from the acting class at the University of Cincinnati to stand on street corners and flag down the first police car they saw. The actor would tell the officer that they found an envelope containing cash and wanted to turn it in. There was an investigator in an unmarked car nearby who would take photos of the envelope being passed and the vehicle equipment number to identify the officer(s) in the cruiser.

The team simultaneously went to all six police districts to run the operation. The next day they went to the District to retrieve the envelopes from their property rooms. Four of the envelopes were intact and contained all of the money. One was not turned in at all and the other had only eight one hundred dollar bills in it was called into the District and immediately was arrested for theft in office which is a felony in Ohio, inconsequential of the amount of the theft. The law applies to any public employee while on duty.

The officer who took the missing envelope was called into the OPSC office and was asked about the whereabouts of the envelope. The officer claimed that it was still in his briefcase and that he had completely forgotten about it. The officer claimed that it was simply a mistake and he had no intention of pocketing the cash. His case was referred to the hearing officer for disciplinary action.

Word of the sting spread throughout the police officer like a flu epidemic. Cops were all running scared that they might be targeted by the rat squad.

***

In their first three months, the team was able to close out all of the prior open cases. Dave established that each team member would spend one day in the office handling incoming complaint calls and that allowed the complainants to speak to a real person.

Dave received a call from the Colerain Township Police Chief asking for the FIT to respond to an officer involved shooting in their jurisdiction. Dave ordered the team to offer any assistance possible, but to use caution interviewing the involved officer because they would not be able to compel answers under the *Garrity Rule*. The shooting occurred atter a short police pursuit. When an officer approached the vehicle from the front, the driver stepped on the gas in an attempt to hit her. She fired a single shot which penetrated the windshield and struck the driver in the head killing him. The team's results were turned over to the Hamilton County prosecutor who determined that the officer's action was both reasonable and necessary and no criminal charges would be forthcoming. The Colerain Township Police, based upon the information provided by the team, determined that the action of the officer was within police department policy and no disciplinary action would be sought.

Robin was on her desk day when she took a call telling her that an officer was working off-duty security jobs and was not paying city income tax for the work. Cincinnati allows its officers to work off-duty in their police uniform if they obtain a permit. Robin called the Detail Coordination Unit and asked what permits the officer had approved. She was told the officer had five approved permits issued for the Cincinnati Reds, Cincinnati Bengals, FC Cincinnati Soccer, the Corryville Business Association and St. Theresa for their bingo and festival.

The sports teams all carry off-duty cops as employees and take out all appropriate taxes so they were a non-issue. She went to St. Theresa and was told that they paid officers in cash and they did not keep records of who worked, so that was a dead end. She went to the Corryville Business Association who told her that the officers were paid in cash at the end of their shift, but they had records of who worked and when.

Robin contacted the City Income Tax bureau and was told that the officer did not claim any work other than employer paid tax, although the Corryville records showed him working forty-two days the previous year. Robin then asked about the other officers working the same detail and was told that only one of the fourteen officers claimed income from the Association.

Robin took the question to Dave who assigned two other investigators to help her with the names on the list. She had the named officer come to the office and told him to bring his union rep or an attorney with him.

When he arrived, she took him and the FOP attorney into a room where a City Income Tax employee was waiting. The tax person pulled his previous filings out of a folder and the records from the Corryville detail. Robin told the officer that failing to declare income was a misdemeanor crime and that he could be terminated from his employment as a result. The officer agreed to pay all the back taxes plus interest and the case was closed.

The other officers on the list provided from Corryville provided a much broader problem. Officers were making thousands of dollars in cash payments from their security work and few were actually declaring it on their annual tax forms. One individual made almost sixty thousand dollars working security and claimed none of the income to city, state or federal tax agencies. His intormaton was referred to the Criminal Division of the Internal Revenue Service and he was indicted by a Federal Grand Jury.

XII

Dave called Robin into his office and told her to go to the residence of a recently fired cop and retrieve all of the city equipment he had been issued. He told her to take Sgt. Wills with her.

The two drove to the house and walked onto the porch of the house. Robin knocked on the front door and a male voice from inside yelled, "Go away!" Robin said, "I am Sgt. Milner and we are here to pick up the equipment that you were supposed to return last month."

There was silence from inside of the house and then a click sound just before the loud blast of the shotgun firing. The lead slug went through the front door and shattered Robin's chest. She slumped to the floor. Wills grabbed her by the shoulders and dragged her out into the yard. He screamed into the radio, "Car 48, SHOTS FIRED, OFFICER DOWN,OFFICERS NEED ASSISTANCE!" The tones that open every police frequency in Greater Cincinnati sounded and the radio cracked, "Attention all cars, all departments, officer needs assistance 1137 Laidlaw Avenue. Report of officer down at that location.

There was silence in the house as the sirens approaching got louder and louder. Communications Section advised, "Attention Car 48, SWAT is en route to your location." Police cars were arriving in droves and the entire block surrounding the house was locked down. A second blast of the shotgun was heard inside of the house and then silence again.

The paramedics arrived while Sgt. Wills was pointing his gun at the front door to protect the officer on the ground. The two medics looked up at Wills and said, "She was dead instantly. The slug blew out her heart." They went to the ambulance and got a white sheet which they put on top of her body. The SWAT van arrived and Wills told the Commander about the second shot and following silence. The Commander made the decision to breech the front door. When the team entered, they saw the former officer leaning against the hallway wall with his brain matter splattered all over the wall and ceiling. It was clear that he had placed the barrel of the shotgun under his chin and fired it.

Dave was in his office when the assistance call went out. He knew the address was where his officers were and ran to his unmarked car. He turned on the lights and siren and drove like a madman to the address. When he approached he could see Sgt. Wills standing over a body covered with a sheet. His stomach turned as he knew that it had to be Robin. He walked up to the body and carefully slid the sheet back far enough to see Robin's face and then carefully covered her again. Tears were streaming down his face as he knew that his friend and colleague was dead.

Homicide detectives and a forensic team arrived and got the photographs of the scene. Officers from multiple districts were arriving in droves and many veteran cops were walking away from the scene crying at the loss of a fellow officer. The Police Chief arrived and ordered that the body of the officer be removed and the ambulance take her to the Coroner's Office with a front and rear police escort. As the three vehicles left the area, cops could be seen standing at attention and saluting their fallen comrade. When the procession reached the Coroner's Lab, there was a line of police vehicles and lines of uniformed and plainclothes cops standing at attention. There were two fire trucks with fireman standing at attention on top ot their rigs and the ladders of the two trucks making a "V" over the driveway in tribute to a fallen hero.

Dave drove across the bridge into Kentucky and went to St. Elizabeth North Hospital. He walked into the Emergency Room and showed his badge to the nurse, asking to talk to Dr. Elaine. When the doctor saw Dave, her face said that she knew why he was there. She led him to a conference room and Dave pulled out a chair for her to sit. Dave said, "You know that Robin was as much a member of my family as she is to you. I hate to have to be the one to tell you that she died in the line of duty today. This is not the time to get into the details of what happened, but she was simply doing her job. I came to be with you and to give you an insight into what will happen." Elaine collapsed into Dave's arms sobbing uncontrollably. Dave held her tightly and whispered, "I loved Robin as much as I love my wife and children. She will always be my hero."

When Elaine somewhat regained her composure Dave said, "Robin has been taken to the Coroner's lab where she will be guarded twenty-four hours a day by two members of the Police Honor Guard. They will be with her when she is moved to a funeral home of your choosing. I know that Robin was not religious, but we can get the

Cintas Center, a basketball arena, which can accommodate ten thousand cops who would like to pay tribute. The Cincinnati Police chaplain will officiate it. This City also wants to pay tribute to a very special woman who made the ultimate sacrifice protecting them. I have been to many police funerals and the response of the public is overwhelming."

"You will be getting a female liason from the Fraternal Order of Police who will help you set up arrangements to bring her and your family into town and will help you through these very difficult times. My wife and I will also be available if you need someone to cry with. Let us all help you get through this.

Dave drove home immediately after he dropped off Elaine and slumped into the arms of his wife.

***

Two members of the Honor Guard protected Robin from the time she arrived at the morgue. They rotated in three hour shifts and moved with the precision of a military unit. The only time she was without the team was when the autopsy was performed with just the pathologist and two homicide detectives present. The pathologist saw the tears in the eyes of the two seasoned detectives who were watching a comrade being disected and told them that the moment the lead slug passed through the sternum, she was dead. It was unlikely that she had the time to feel any pain. Immediately after the autopsy was completed, Robin was taken to a waiting ambulance and transported to the largest funeral home in the City of Cincinnati. It was escorted by police motorcyles from Cincinnati, University of Cincinnati, Hamilton, Butler, Warren and Clermont County Sheriff units. When the procession arrived at the funeral home, there were nearly one hundred cops in uniform from multiple agencies in two lines standing at attention and saluting the flag draped guerney.

***

Dave arrived at the funeral home at noon the next day. The visitation was scheduled from four until eight with the private FOP service at noon. Only the elected officers of the FOP would be present for it.

Dave and Elaine were alone with the casket when Elaine said, "I have something Robin would want you to see." She lifted her dress showing her bare ass and on the right cheek was a tattoo saying, "Robin's forever." Dave now understood the bond that the two women had. Neither had any semblence of fear of anything.

At the conclusion of the thirty minute FOP service, the funeral director walked up to Dave and told him that the line outside the door was approximately one thousand people. When Dave relayed that to Elaine, she asked if the service could start immediately. There were three chairs that everyone would pass getting to the half open casket. Robin had been dressed in her dress uniform with her sergeant stripes visible and her white hat laying on her chest. The chairs were for Elaine and Robin's parents, who had flown in from Florida. Elaine asked that Dave stand behind the three to provide support. Dave told Elaine to look at the patches of the police uniforms that passed by and she would see the bond between law enforcement officers from all over the world. People would stop for just a moment to console the seated family . A man walked up and said, "I have been sent to pass along our sorrow from the thirteen thousand members of the Los Angeles Police Department." Another said, "Thiry-nine thousand members of the New York City Police Department want you to know that you are in our thoughts and prayers." As the line passed by, Elaine saw uniforms from the Metropolitan Police of London, Madrid, Aukland, New South Wales, Montreal, Toronto and the Royal Canadian Mounted Police. All fifty states were represented and a cop from Honolulu stopped and said, "The police in Hawaii send condolences."

Eight o'clock came and the funeral director said there was still a line out the door and wanted to know whether to shut the visitation down. Elaine asked that it be kept open until the last person who wanted to came through. It was nine-thirty when the doors were closed and locked.

***

The hearse was escorted to the campus of Xavier University. The basketball court of the Cintas Center was covered with a tarp and seating for several hundred was in place. The rest of the facility was opened to the public.

The police academy recruit class was formed in two lines down the sidewalk leading to the street level entrance to the arena. The recruits stood at attention saluting. As the casket passed each pair of recruits dropped their right hand to their side in unity. Dave was asked to be a pall bearer, but declined, telling Elaine that the team would be unified and precise in the movement to the service. The honor guard team was waiting inside to stand guard over the casket.

All four local television stations ran the service live. They each had an experienced law enforcement officer to provide commentary about the process of paying tribute to a fallen officer.

The facility quickly filled to capacity and everyone stood as the casket was wheeled into the arena. The family was put up on the stage behind the casket and Elaine wanted Dave and his family to be up there with them.

The first speaker was the Mayor of the City of Cincinnati who spoke about the gratitude of the City for Robin's service. He was followed by the Police Chief who spoke of Robin's distnguished career of service. Then it was Dave's turn to speak. He said, "My name is Lt. Dave Bristol and I was the Commander of Robin's unit. But Robin was much more than just a member of my team. She was a friend and a role model to me. We met when we were teamed up in District One and we became known as 'Batman and Robin.' That was caused by her devotion to the protection of the people of Cincinnati. When I got promoted, we were split up. She moved to District Five where she continued to serve and protect. She got promoted and immediately earned the respect of the people who served under her. When I got promoted to Lieutenant and took over the new unit, Robin was the first person I asked to join me. Robin had been injured more than once in the line of duty, once getting stabbed on Fountain Square. But she always bounced back. The circumstances leading to her death will never make any sense because she was only at that house to pick up a box of equipment from a former police officer. It was as simple as it gets, but that routine situation cost her life. I will always love Robin as much as I love my wife and my children and she will forever live in my heart. Cincinnati Police officers will forever try to live up to the bar she set. Rest in peace Robin, we are here to continue your work."

Tears were flowing freely as Dave walked back to his seat.

***

After the service was concluded everyone in attendance stood as the casket left the arena. Outside, the line of over three hundred police vehicles waited patiently to take Robin to her final resting place. The twelve mile trek required the shutting down of major streets. The streets were lined on both sides by people waving American flags and bringing their children to watch. In the suburban communities the procession passed through, fire trucks were parked with their ladders crossed and police and American flags draped from the ladders. The firefighters stood on top of their apparatus standing at attention and saluting in tribute.

The procession was three miles long and was led by motorcycle cops completely encircling the hearse. When the procession entered the cemetary, it passed under two City of Spingdale fire trucks hanging the blue line flag in mid-air.

The cars had to park in up to a mile away and walk to the cemetary delaying the service to accommodate them. When the officers got into lines on the hillsides surrounding the burial site, the service began. The all county tones broadcast over the police radio frequencies and over a loud speaker at the cemetary. Cincinnati Police Communications broadcast, "Attention all cars, all departments. Attempting to contact Car 49, Sgt. Robin Milner. Sgt. Milner, please respond. No response, Sgt. Milner is out of service. May she eternally rest in peace." That was followed by the playing of Taps and the officers were dismissed.

After all of the officers left the area, there was a short farewell from Robin's parents, Elaine and Dave's family.

XIII

The first thing Dave did when he went back into his office was hang an eighteen by twenty-four inch framed photo of Robin's coffin being pulled out of the hearse. Every morning he would stop and get his cup of coffee and then walk up to the photo, placing his hand on the glass to have Robin give him the strength to get through the day.

For the next three months, Dave's enthusiam continued to decline. He had a great staff that were working their cases dilligently, but all Dave was seeing was, at first an empty desk that Robin sat in and then someone else in Robin's chair.

Dave called the Chief's secretary to get an appointment to see him and she was able to get him an hour. Dave walked into the Chief's office, sat down and said, "Chief. I cannot do this anymore. I need to resign. Every day I walk past the desk that Sgt. Milner sat at, I want to cry. I have a great staff that works hard and I do not have the energy to lead them." There was silence in the room until the Chief asked, "How much time do you have before you can retire Dave?" Dave answered, "I am forty-eight years old, so I have the age. I need eighteen months to have the twenty-five years to draw a pension." The Chief thought for a moment and asked, "How about if I were to tranfer you, is there anywhere you would like to be?" Dave got a sad look on his face and said, "I am not sure I can be enthusiatic anywhere in the department, sir"

There was another short period of silence and the Chief's face seemed to light up. He said, "How about I make you the Commander of the Police Academy. You will help mold the future of this department? There is a Captain's examination coming up that would help increase your pension and I could name you as the head of the Training Unit. Would that work?"

Dave answered, "Actually, that might work. I could introduce them to the bar that Sgt. Milner set and help them reach it."

***

Dave moved into his new office at the Police Training facility which was formerly the practice center for the Cincinnati Bengals pro football team. It was an area large enough to offer the ability to conduct both reality and scenario based training. There was not a current class of police recruits and the recruiting unit was screening candidates for the next class. Dave was required to be approved by the Ohio Peace Officer Training Commission which meant attending a Commander training program.

The recruit class had forty-five students. They walked into the classroom which had their names on their desk and two large boxes. The first box contained their uniform shirts, pants and hats. The second contained five four inch binders which the students would fill before the training was completed.

Dave walked into the room in his uniform and all eyes were on him. He began his remarks with, "From this point forward, you will jump out of your seats every time that door opens. Does not matter whether it is the Mayor, the Police Chief, me or the janitor. You will stand until told to be seated as a sign of respect to the people who enter this room. When you walked down the hallway to come here, you passed a wall of heroes. These are people who sat in the same seats as you occupy now and they gave their lives in service to the citizens of Cincinnati. I know of the loss felt because a partner of mine is on that wall. Sgt. Robin Milner was murdered by a man who graduated from this police adademy. She was not prepared for a confrontation. All she was at his house to do was pick up a box containing the uniforms and equipment that he disgraced."

"Some of you believe that we have an obligation to make you successful. Those that do will not be here on graduation day. Others believe that since they completed a college degree, this will be a piece of cake. You will likely not be here either. You will complete a four year degree in six months, so be prepared to work your ass off. You will take individual tests for defensive tactics, emergency driving, first aid and firearms. If you fail any of those tests, you will fail the program. You will take a single written examination on all of the other topics. If you fail that test, you fail the complete program. On your desk was a box containing binders. You will fill all of them and they will be scored. If you fail to complete the binders, you fail the entire program."

Fot those of you who are employed by the City of Cincinati, the cost of your training is approximately fifty thousand dollars. The City hates to waste its money. For those of you who are employed by other police agencies, you will adhere to the same rules as the Cincinnati cops. If you do not follow those rules, we cannot fire you. However, when we toss you out of the class, your agency will fire you so fast that your head will spin."

Our goal is not whether you successfully complete the academy. It is to give you the necessary tools and skills to survive after the last time you walk out of this classroom."

"The instructors are here to help you. All you have to do is ask. I am here to help you. All you have to do is ask. Prepare to work hard and pay attention. We are here for you and I wish you success in your journey to be a law enforcement officer."

***

At the end of the first month, the class had reduced by four. Three voluntarily left, making the decision that law enforcement was simply not the career for them. The fourth, a twenty-three year old male, was brought into Dave's office after being found in the women's locker room where he was watching the female recruits shower and dress. Dave looked at the scared young man and said, "What a waste! You not only screwed up your career aspirations, you probably ruined your life as well. You are under arrest for Voyeurism, a misdemeanor under Ohio law, but it also carries a designation as a low level sex offender. Handcuff him and transport him to the Justice Center."

Half way thru the twenty-eight week class, two more left the class. One female was unable to pass the firearm portion even though three instructors worked tirelessly to help her. She had a paralyzing fear of the weapon and presented an imminent danger to everyone around her. The other simply quit showing up for class and never gave a reason. All of the items he was issued were found sitting outside the front entrance to the facility when the first person arrived to open the doors.

***

At the graduation ceremony, Dave stood in front of a room full of family and friends of the recruits and said, "These men and women have successfully completed the most rigorous programs imaginable. They are now ready to go out and protect and serve the residents, workers and visitors to the community they are assigned. They could not have accomplished this monumental task without the support of their family and friends. The people in this room are the reason that they are up on this stage today."

XIV

Dave turned his attention to the Captain's examination. He obtained the books from which the test would be created from the public library and turned his kitchen table into a study desk. His family would come by and bring him coffee and cookies and tell him he would ace it. It was a real confidence builder.

The results of the written examination were posted and Dave finished first on the list. He received a phone call from the Chief who told him, "I will be announcing my retirement next month and I want my last official act to be assigning you to the position of Captain of the training unit. That should keep you occupied until you have the time in to retire."

The training unit of the police department consisted of the police academy, firearms unit, police recruiting and advanced training unit. Each was distinct but intertwined with the other units. Dave met with each commander to identify areas that he could help them develop better officers.

***

Dave finally had accumulated the twenty-five years that he needed to retire with sixty-six percent of his top three years salary. Now he needed to decide what he wanted to do after he left the police department. He was sitting in his office when the secretary told him he had a called from the now retired police chief. He was told, "Dave, Cincinnati Children's Hospital system is looking for an Executive Vice

President of their Safety and Security Department and I gave them your name to consider.

Two days later when he arrived home, his wife gave him a message that the hospital had called. The next morning he returned the call and was told that he was one of the five finalists for the position and that he would be interviewed the following day.

When Dave walked into the conference room in the Executive office, he saw two women and one man seated at the table across from him. Dave sat in a chair across from them and the male opened the discussion with, "My name is Donald Watson and I am the Chief Executive Officer of the Cincinnati Children's Hospital system. To my left is Donna Murray, who is the Vice President of Operations. To her right is Wendy Walker, Vice President of Human Resources. We thank you for coming and participating in this process. Here is how it will work, Each of us will ask one question and we will continue until there are no more questions. Let me begin with this question. What is your biggest accomplishment with Cincinnati Police?"

Dave thought for a moment and answered, "Cincinnati Police gave me the opportunity and pleasure of working with the best police officers in this country. I also got the chance to serve the citizens of Cincinnati and to keep them safe. That is my biggest accomplishment."

Donna Murray asked, "Without getting into specifics because you are not familiar with our operation, what do you see the function of the security department to be?"

Dave answered, "I see four areas of focus in this order. The first is the safety of the children who need medical issues resolved. The second is the employees who provide the medical services to the children. The third is the family and visitors to the hospital and the fourth is the facility itself.

Wendy Walker asked, "What is it that you would look for in an employee?" Dave paused and said, "I would want people who have the same training as any police officer in the State of Ohio. There are several reasons for that. The first is that they are trained to handle high-stress situations and they understand their limitations under the law. They are trained in specific methodologies to diffuse difficult situations. I am a proponent of armed officers, but that is a decision which comes from the corporate level. Being fully trained also reduces the liabilty of the hospital in a civil litigation."

Donald Murray asked, "So you would want your officers to have full police powers?" Dave answered, "The hospital would form a public safety division and be able to make officers sworn peace officers, I think that gives the officers more options. By that I mean that they do not need to involve police jurisdictions in an action because they are limited in their capabilities. It would not be a priority in the operation of the safety of the hospital and there would likely be less than twenty arrests per year,"

Donna Murray asked, "Where do you see the need for resources to be focused?"

Dave responded, "First and foremost is the Emergency Department. It is where children are brought when they are in distress and the parents bringing them are emotionally stressed. The visibility and demeanor of the officers can serve to difuse some of the stress and allow the medical professionals to provide the care the child needs. Second is the parking areas. They provide a place for predators to commit robbery or sexual assault. Once again, visibility serves as a detrrent to criminal activity. Third is the main entrance where most of the people will enter and the visibility of the uniform sets the stage for polite interaction with the employees. Fourth is the Security Office where cameras can be monitored, calls for service can be received, people can enter to report incidents and supervisors can perform their function."

Wendy Walker asked, "Why would you want to leave Cincinnati Police?" Dave answered, "Less than one year ago I attended the funeral of a female police sergeant who was killed in the line of duty. She was my partner when we were both street cops working downtown and was much more than just a partner. She was a member of my family just as much as my wife and children. She worked for me and I assigned her the call that caused her death. That was devastating and it is time for me to move on from it and utilize my training and skill in a different capacity."

Donald Murray asked, What do you see of role of the securty department is with regard to employees?" Dave responded, "That is a multi-level question. First, I think the department needs to provide training on active shooter situations, mass casualty and personal safety. It also needs to set guidelines on internal theft and narcotics controls."

Murray said, "That ends our questions for the interview. You are the final applicant to be interviewed and we will make a decision within the next three days. Thank you for coming.

***

Dave went to the office to complete his day. He would tell his wife that he did not get any vibe from the interview as to how he fared.

***

Dave drove home wondering about his presentation in the interview. The three people who conducted it left no impression as to how he had done.

He was readying to go to bed when his cell phone rang, It was a call from Police Communications telling him that a recruit was transported to the University of Cincinnati Medical Center by the Evendale, Ohio paramedic squad from injuries received in a training accident. Dave dressed quickly and drove to UC Medical Center. When he arrived at the hospital he found two Assistant Police Chiefs and a Sergeant from the Firearm Training Unit already there. The Sergeant told Dave that the female officer was in surgery and that her injury was significant. He told Dave that they were conducting night fluid (full speed) training and that the female recruit was shot with Simunition. He explained that Simuntion is ammunition with a paper wad for a projectile and does not penetrate skin. Dave ordered the Sergeant to have a police car pick up the family of the recruit and to bring them to the hospital. He also ordered the suspension of simunition training pending the results of the investigation and called the Force Investigation Team commander and told him to take his whole team to the firing range to start the investigation. He told the commander to have a preliminary report on his desk by eight o'clock in the morning.

After five hours, the surgeon came out and told the officers in the waiting room, "The officer suffered internal injuries from the concusion of the simunition round striking her above the kidney. We had to remove her spleen which was damaged beyond repair. She will never be able to work as a police officer again and it will be forty-eight hours before we are out of the woods. She is in extremely critical condition."

Dave left the hospital and went straight to his office to attempt to get the full story. He was reading the statements of the trainer who fired the shot that said, "We were involved in a struggle for the .357 magnum revolver I had and it fired when I forced her arm behind her back. She screamed in pain and I immeidately called for a paramedic unit. The round did not penetrate her shirt and there was no blood. The paramedic unit arrived six minutes later and transported her to the hospital."

The FIT report indicated there were four instructors and four recruits involved in the training. The rest of the recruits were inside the building waiting their turn to do the training. None of the people present saw anything because they were involved in their own training.

***

Dave was sitting in his office when his personal cell phone rang. The caller was the Vice President of Human Resources telling him that the position was his if he still wanted it. She set up a time to meet to explain the salary and benefit package to him. The position would pay ninety thousand dollars per year and he would be incorporated into their healthcare program.

Dave explained that he would need four weeks to provide notice to the City of Cincinnati and file his retirement paperwork with the pension board.

Dave wrote a resignation letter and hand delivered it to the Police Chief. He then made the one hundred mile drive to Columbus, Ohio to the state pension board where he filled out his retirement forms. When he returned to the office, Dave met with the staff of the Training Academy so they could hear firsthand of his leaving. He thanked each member of his staff for their loyalty and work ethic and wished them all well.

On his last day at the Academy, he was greeted with a cake and a ton of hugs from the staff. He was told that there would be a retirement party for him at a restaurant called Lucious Q's and that his attendance with his family was mandatory.

Dave, his wife and their three children arrived at the restaurant to find over three hundred people already there. The retired Police Chief, as well as cops he had worked with twenty-five years ago lavished him with praise and did their best to embarrass him as the evening progressed with speakers talking about working with him.

Dave's wife hugged him and cried as the accolades were given.

XV

Dave met with the Chief Executive Officer of the Hospital system and was told he had the freedom to institute whatever changes he felt necessary to improve the service the Security Department provided. He was then given a tour of the base hospital and shown to his new office where he met Sandy, his new secretary.

His first act was to hang the picture of Robin on the wall. The office was the size of the Cincinnati Police Chief and his desk was real cherry wood and spacious. He sat alone for several minutes just taking in the enormity of the situation until Sandy entered with a pot of coffee for him.

Dave wrote a resolution for the Board to approve declaring the Security Department as a full fledged law enforcement agency and then delivered it to the CEO. He then went to work on an organizational chart which would consist of one Captain, who would serve as Assistant Chief and command the staff at the base hospital. The three satelite facilities would be commanded by a Liuetenant who would each have three shift sergeants. He would also have three investigators who would work out of the base hospital, but investigate crimes at all of the locations.

Dave asked Sandy to contact the Director of the Nationwide Children's Hospital in Columbus, Ohio to take a tour of their operation. Sandy came back and told Dave that the Chief of Nationwide suggested Dave spend three days in Columbus and he would show Dave how their system operates.

Dave met with the commanders of the four facilities and told them about the transition to a Police Department as well as shared the new organizational chart. He told them everyone would have one year to obtain certification as a Peace Officer in Ohio and that Children's would pay for the training, but not the time of the officer. At the conclusion of the meeting, two of the supervisors told him they were unwilling to take the training and would be resigning. Dave thanked them for their honesty and wished them well in their future endeavors.

Dave made a trip to each of the satellite sights to find out what they were experiencing. After the last visit, Dave sat and wrote a specific plan for each center, focusing attention on the Emergency Department and the front entrance.

***

Dave pulled into the parking lot of Nationwide Children's Hospital just before eight in the morning. Cincinnati Children's made a reservation for him at a downtown Columbus hotel for his three day look at the security operation of Nationwide.

Dave walked into the large lobby of the facility and immediately saw two uniformed officers in different corners. He walked up to the closest officer and said, "I have a meeting with your Chief this morning." The young cop smiled and replied, "You must be the Director from Cincinnati." He turned away and said something into his portable radio. Dave could not hear the radio because it was muted by an earplug in the officer's ear. The officer said, "He asks you wait here and he will be down in a couple of minutes." A few minutes later Dave saw a grey haired man in a suit walking quickly toward him. The man extended his hand and said, "I am Phillip Hall and I am the Director of Police Services for Nationwide Children's Hospital System, follow me please. Hall led Dave to an elevator and they went to the third floor. When the elevator door opened, Dave saw a large sign saying "P O L I C E" above the entrance. They walked to a door and the female behind the glass buzzed the door open for them. The two walked down a long hallway passing small rooms which Hall said were interview and interrogation rooms. They arrived at a door which required Hall to use his key card to gain entry. They walked into a large room with a male seated at a console and the wall full of small television sets displaying different views.

Hall told Dave, "This is our central command center. The screens are displaying real-time views of all of the surveillance cameras at all of our facilities. All 9-1-1 calls made from our campuses come directly here. If the caller calls 9-9-1-1, the call goes to the dispatch center that serves them." As they stood and watched, the 9-1-1 line rang. The male took the call and then broadcast, "300 units, caller reports a fight between two males in the rear parking lot. Units responding identify." The man then loaded the camera onto the large screen and the three were able to watch the fight as well as the arrival of officers. Hall told Dave that the video feeds from all cameras is saved to the cloud, but were not available to public scrutiny as the hospital is not a public entity and is not subject to Freedom of Information Act or Public

Records Law. They were only kept for thirty days and then deleted unless they were needed as evidence.

Hall said, "We are directly hooked into Ohio's Law Enforcement Automated Data System to allow us to do warrant checks from here. We arrested eighteen people on open warrants last year. Warrant service is not counted in our annual arrest statistics as we only hold them until the agency responsible comes and picks them up." One of the two combatants had an open warrant from Whitehall Police and was handcuffed. The dispatcher called Whitehall PD to come pick him up. Hall said, "I tell all of my officers that arrest is the last option and they do not get points for the number of arrests they make."

He continued, "All of our facilities are assigned a radio number. 100 is the base and so on. The commander is the 00 number, the sergeants are 80 numbers and the posts all have their own number." Hall looked at the dispatcher and said, "Tell 200 to activate his emergency button." He looked at Dave and said, "Each of our radios is equipped with a panic button to use in case they are unable to speak." When the button was activated, the computer screen lit up in red with EMERGENCY flashing on it. Below that was the officer assigned to that radio and their current location so that assitance could be immediately sent.

They stayed in the command center for a short time and Hall motioned Dave to the door. They went down the hallway and Hall opened another door into a large office with five desks. Hall said, "This is our investigators office. All criminal investigations system wide are conducted from here. The investigators are also responsible for coducting background investigations on new employees and to issue their key cards after employment. Each investigator is assigned a day to take employee photos and issue their id badges." The two walked into the office of the supervisor and Hall told the man behind the desk, "Tell us what open investigations we have." The supervisor pulled out a folder and listed the active cases they were working on. They included two drug diversion cases, three theft cases and an aggravated assault that occurred in the parking garage.

The two went to lunch in the hospital cafeteria and Hall told Dave, "I retired as a Lieutenant from Columbus PD where I was the commander of the SWAT team. The SWAT program is one of a few in the country that has no other responsibilites other than tactial operations such as high risk warrant and drug raids and requests from the street cops for a tactical response. That experience taught me there are multiple ways of resolving a situation without the use of force."

After lunch Hall took Dave to a conference room where there were multiple binders laying on the large table. Hall told Dave, "I have two meetings that I could not get out of. You will find all of the information about our operation in the binders. Write any questions you have and I will try to answer them when I return. Dave found a hot pot of coffee and cups on the sink and sat down to get to work. The first binder was the arrests made by the department for the previous year. It showed that there were twenty-eight total arrests, of which twenty were for felony offenses. A deeper dive showed seven were for felony domestic violence, nine were for felony weapons offenses which included having weapons under disability and carrying a concealed loaded firearm. Two were for felony drug offenses, one for felony theft and one for felony assault on a police officer. After the statistics page was a detailed report on each of the cases, some of which had multiple charges involved in a single arrest.

Next, Dave looked at the budget for the department for the previous year. When Dave looked at the cost of salary and benefits, he cringed at the thought of getting his board to agree.

Last came the focus on the policy and procedure manual which was two hundred and forty pages It detailed the conduct and actions that was expected of officers of all ranks. Dave made a note to ask for a copy of the manual to use as a guideline for his staff

When Hall came back into the room, Dave said, "I am mentally exhausted. That was a boatload of information." Hall smiled and said, "We will get together to discuss any issues after you see the operation of the satellite sites tomorrow. Go to your hotel and relax, Tomorrow will be just as busy."

***

The following morning Dave made the first of his five stops at the satellite facilities in the Nationwide system. At each location, he was given a tour of the various locations where officers were assigned by the site commander, who also explained the types of interactions that his officers encountered. Dave was able to see four of the sites and scheduled the last one for his last day in town.

When he returned to the base operation, Dave and Hall went to the places where the officers were assigned and stood and watched them in action. It gave Dave an understanding of what the rationale was for placement and how the visibility of a uniform police officer kept emotions to a minimum.

Hall sent Dave home with a full copy of the Policy and Procedure Manual to provide a guide for Cincinnati's operation.

***

When Dave got back into his office, he began the laborous work of putting together a package to submit to the Board for their approval. He began by assembling the numbers for a budget. He became very nervous when the first numbers he crunched were for the salary and benefits of the staff. The sworn personnel only came in at just over four million dollars annually, Then another one million in equipment for the operation: including the purchase of sixty .40 caliber Glock handguns and two high capacity magazines at a cost of eight hundred dollards each; tactical vests at seven hundred and fifty dollars each; Tasers at nine hundred dollars each; cost for police academy training for current employees at twenty-five hundred dollars each; and three fully equipped police cars at fifty thousand dollars.

Stage two of the process was to prepare a Standard Operating Procedure Manual that would detail the guidelines for the behavior and directions that the officers would follow in their day to day operations. Dave read every page of the document used in Columbus, incorporating much of the policy into the manual for Cincinnati.

He anticipated that it would take a full year to transition into a fully operational police department.

XVI

Dave had other issues he needed to resolve. Two of his facility commanders declined to attend the police academy and needed to be replaced with certified peace officers. Another twelve of the current staff indicated that they did not wish to complete the training and would be seeking employment elsewhere.

Dave was shocked when the Board unanimously approved the package he submitted, including the budget,without any changes. Dave would later come to find out that the CEO of the hospital told the Board that he had full faith in Dave and asked the Board to give Dave the freedom to get the job done.

Dave made inquiries to the three regional police training academies in the Cincinnati area to try to recruit officers to join his team. He also got word to Sheriff's deputies who worked in Corrections but were certified as peace officers so they could transport prisoners and be armed. Those efforts got him nine new officers. He was beginning to get it together.

***

Dave was up for his one year evaluation and felt that he had not yet accomplished all of the things he needed to. He was in his office when he received a call to report to the CEO where he was handed his evaluation which gave him "exceeds expectations" in most of the areas. The CEO offered him a three year extention of his contract and Dave quickly signed it.

With the house now empty of kids, Dave and his wife were able to focus on their own lives. Their oldest son was now a bailiff with the Hamilton County Municipal Court Criminal Division, their daughter was a pediatric dentist and their youngest son got his real estate license. The combination of his police pension and the new job allowed Dave to pay all of the costs of their college and none had any loan debt as they moved out and on.

For the first time since starting the new job, Dave felt comfortable taking a vacation. He and his wife decided to drive to central Ohio in Amish country to get away from the hustle and bustle of the city. It was a four hour drive, but once they got onto the side roads, they could feel the peace and serenity of the country life. When they arrived at the bed and breakfast, they were taken to a room with a patio that overlooked a large farm field with a single tractor doing laps to cultivate it. They sat on a porch swing and heard the absolute sounds of silence and they soaked in all of the tranquillity.

The desk clerk told them that only one pizza shop was open for business on Sunday and that only a limited number were open on Monday. Those were the Amish days of rest. The decided to just drive until they found a restaurant for dinner, and there was one in Berlin, Ohio. The only traffic they saw was Amish on motorized bicycles and horse drawn black carriages. They spent four days cruising the area and just enjoying each other's company.

When they returned home, Dave felt renewed and refreshed. Dave unlocked the front door and saw a footprint on the mail laying on the floor of the foyer. He had stopped delivery of the daily newspaper, but the mail slot was in the front door, so it was not necessary to put a hold on the mail. Dave called Cincinnati Police and an officer responded. There was nothing out of place, but clearly someone had entered the house.

The cop who came to take the report called for detectives since there was actually physical evidence. It took about twenty minutes for the detectives to arrive and both knew Dave from his time in the training unit. They bagged the piece of mail with the shoe print and walked around the house to look for more evidence. Dave took them to a bedroom closet where he kept a small safe which did not appear to have been opened. They took fingerprints off the door and Dave told them that he had installed a Ring door camera. They watched the video and saw a white male walk up to the front door and pick the lock open.

The detectives ran facial recognition against the Ohio Bureau of Motor Vehicles database and came up with a hit on a man named Bob Whorly. Whorly had a previous criminal record for breaking and entering. They ran his credit card and found that he had just checked into a motel on the outskirts of Nashville, Tennessee. The detectives drove to the Clerk of Courts and signed warrants for breaking and entering and attempted safecracking and then faxed the warrants to the Nashville Metro Police Department, asking them to pick Whorly up at his motel. Nashville Metro found Whorly and arrested him without incident, but he refused to allow police to search his car. Police towed his car to their impound lot and obtained a search warrant from a judge there. The search revealed a high-end Nikkon camera worth $2,500 and several credit cards in multiple names.

The two Cincinnati detectives made the five hour drive to Nashville to interview Whorly in the Davidson County, Tennessee jail and to be present at his extradition hearing. Whorly waived his right to a hearing and was brought back to Cincinnati by the detectives.

***

Dave was sitting at his desk reading the incident reports from the satellite locations when his private office line phone rang. The caller was the commander of the Cincinnati Police gang unit who told Dave that two rival gang members had been shot and were being transported to Children's base. He told Dave that there was a likelihood of retaliation in the hospital.

Dave doubled the uniformed officers in the Emergency Department and ordered both the Sergeant and the Captain to oversee the operation. He assigned an investigator to each of the bangers. A sixteen year old Latin Kings member had life threatening injuries from a gunshot wound to the chest. A fourteen year old was a member of the Price Hills Boyz who suffered a minor gunshot wound to his right arm. Each was accompanied by an entourage of gang members, but they were stopped at the entrance to the ER because they were not eighteen and were told to leave.

The fourteen year old was treated and released, but the sixteen year old needed to be stabilized before being taken into surgery. He was moved to the Intensive Care

Unit and the surgery was scheduled for the following day. He was assigned a twenty-four hour security detail to prevent an attack. The next morning Dave got another call from the gang commander telling him that the unit had received information about an attack which would take place in the hospital when the patient was moved to surgery. Dave assigned two uniforms to supervise the move which would involve taking an elevator up two floors to the surgical unit. A uniformed officer was detailed to the lobby floor to close off one elevator for the move. The gang unit set up two teams of officers to be outside the entrances to the lobby and one reported a beat up vehicle containing four males entering the lot. Three young men got out and walked toward the entrance, while the driver sat with the car running. One team of gang cops followed the three men into the lobby while the other team removed the driver from the car. When the driver was searched, the cops found a loaded nine millimeter handgun in his belt. The three men took an elevator to the fifth floor. The patient was pushed down a hallway with the two uniformed officers in front and behind. As they crossed another hallway, the two cops saw three men in long jackets walking up toward them. When the gurney passed the opening, the two uniforms spun around just in time to see the gang cops holding the three men at gunpoint. With four guns pointed at them, the three gang members dropped to their knees and placed their hands behind their heads. Each was searched and a loaded gun was found on each. The three were handcuffed and taken to the lobby where the commander called for four marked cruisers so that the prisoners could be transported separately to the gang office without being able to communicate with each other.

The four suspects were taken to the gang office and placed in chairs in the waiting room. They were told that, if they tried to talk to each other, they would have soapy washcloths stuffed in their mouths. They were taken, one at a time, to an interrogation room where a man in a three piece suit was waiting. The man introduced himself as a federal prosecutor from the U.S. Attorney Office for the Southern District of Ohio and that he planned to charge each with crimes that would result in significant prison time with the "big boys." His tactic was successful as all four gave the same address to find the rest of the gang members.

The gang commander got a search warrant for the address and called the SWAT team to make entry into the residence. SWAT hit the front and back doors simultaneously surprising the nine gang members in the house. The search revealed drugs, weapons and sixty thousand dollars in cash. When things quieted down, the gang commander called Dave and told him that all of the gang was in custody and he could pull the protection on the rival gang member. The commander also told Dave about the result of the search apologizing that Children's was not eligible for a cut of the cash seizure since it is not a governmental entity. Dave laughed and thanked the gang unit for their help.

XVII

Dave loved going to work each day. His staff was out performing their tasks without causing friction. Dave received compliments from the nurses who told him that they felt safe walking to and from the parking and appreciated seeing the red and blue lights flashing as they approached.

Dave was concerned that the turnover of staff was an ongoing issue, but it was one that he expected as they moved on to municipal law enforcement jobs. Two former members were currently enrolled in the Cincinnati Police Academy and four others had secured positions with high paying suburban police departments.

***

Dave was at home watching television with his wife just before the eleven o'clock news and bedtime when his cell phone rang. The caller was the supervisor at the Liberty Center facility who told Dave that there had been a shooting in the waiting room of the Emergency Department. Dave quickly dressed and ran out of the door to the take-home car the Medical Center provided him. Dave sped down the streets to downtown Cincinnati and then got onto Interstate 75 for the twenty-five mile trip. He had just crossed into Butler County when he saw a set of headlights come on in the median of the Interstate. He looked down at the speedometer and saw that he was traveling at just over ninety miles per hour. The trooper was gaining ground as Dave watched through the rear view mirror and he saw the trooper activate his overhead blue lights. Dave reached down to the toggle switch activating the red and blue strobes in the front grille and back deck to illuminate. He next turned on the siren of the unmarked car and watched as the overhead lights behind him were turned off and the trooper pulled off to the shoulder. Dave left the emergency equipment on until he entered the long private road leading to the hospital. As he approached the Emergency entrance, he saw television news live trucks from both Cincinnati and Dayton parked in the grass with tripods and cameras aimed at the entrance. Dave pulled up in front of the entrance and exposed his badge hanging on a lanyard. He walked over to the officer standing next to the Medical Center cruiser and told him, "Take the cruiser out and inform the media trucks that this is private property and that they have twenty minutes to leave the property or we will tow their vehicles. Turn on the overhead lights and let them see the red and blues."

Dave walked to the front entrance where two Butler County deputies were guarding the front door. The deputies saw the badge and spread apart allowing Dave to enter. When he walked into the waiting area, Dave saw the body of a male in a pool of blood laying on the floor and an older male sitting in a chair. The rest of the waiting area was empty. The shift sergeant walked up to Dave and said, "Here is what we know as of now. The male on the floor was screaming at a woman we believe to be his wife. The officer stationed there was approaching when the subject pulled out a hunting knife and put it to the woman's neck. Before our officer had time to react, the old man sitting in the chair pulled a gun and fired a single shot into the suspect's head. He immediately sat down and laid the gun in his lap, raising his hands above his head. Our officer retrieved the weapon and the old man told him that he is a retired Police Captain from Hamilton Police. A doctor and two nurses were there within seconds trying to administer aid, but the doctor told me the subject was dead before his body hit the floor. I immediately closed the waiting room and moved the people waiting to the Ambulance Entrance and then, as we are not equipped to handle this type of event, called the Butler County Sheriff and asked them to send their homicide investigators. They arrived about fifteen minutes ago.

As soon as the sergeant walked away, the officer assigned to the patrol vehicle walked in and told Dave, "The media said they will leave as soon as someone from the hospital comes out and gives them a statement."

Dave walked out and looked into the grass seeing a bank of microphones set up and flood lights illuminating the area. He walked up to the bank of microphones and stood motionless for a few seconds allowing the media to get their cameras running. He said, "Good evening, my name is Dave Bristol and I am the Director of Police Services for the Children's Medical Center System. I have a short statement after which I will not be taking any questions. Just before eleven o'clock a man in the waiting room of the Emergency Department pulled out a hunting knife and put it to a woman's throat. The man was then shot by a retired Hamilton Police Captain and is deceased. The waiting area is closed off as a crime scene and the investigation is being handled by the Sheriff's office. We anticipate that the Emergency entrance will be re-opened within the next hour. There will no further updates coming from the hospital. All inquiries should be referred to the Butler County Sheriff or Butler County Prosecutor. With that, Dave turned and walked back toward the entrance. He stopped and turned around to see the media packing their equipment and loading their trucks. Dave walked back to the patrol officer and ordered him to park out near the trucks and make sure they parked on the public sidewalk or on the street, making them the County's problem.

Dave walked back to the entrance just as a white van parked. It was marked BUTLER COUNTY CORONER and two men wearing county jail overalls opened the back door and pulled out a gurney and a black body bag, walking in the entrance. They carefully placed the man's body into the bag and placed it on the gurney. The two Sheriff's detectives escorted the old man, who was not in handcuffs, out the front entrance followed by the body. Dave told his sergeant to contact building maintenance to clean the floor so the waiting room could be re-opened and then left to return home

***

Dave walked into the office the next morning and his secretary handed him the final incident report for the event the day before. It provided a timeline and listed the witnesses as well as the statement of the hospital officer present.

Dave was reading it when he received a call from the hospital C.E.O. who told him that hospital policy forbids statements to the media except from the Communications Section, but the exigence of the event caused a departure from that policy. The C.E.O. told Dave that he watched the press conference and that Dave had handled it with professionalism and made the hospital look good. It also took the hospital off the hook for further information and put the onus on the county to update the media. Dave told him that the credit for the resolution of the event should be given to the shift sergeant who oversaw the initial response.

XVIII

Dave was approaching the end of his contract extension and a new five year contract was laying on his desk. He had read it several times, but had not yet signed it.

He left the office and drove seventy miles to the largest recreational vehicle dealer in the Midwest located in Richmond, Indiana. A salesman showed him several RV's and he purchased a new one for ninety thousand dollars. The salesman told him that it would be ready for pickup in three days and he would receive a call as soon as it was ready. Dave drove home and did not tell his wife about the purchase.

Dave was at work when the call came and he immediately left and drove home. He walked into the house and told his wife they needed to go and pick up something, but did not tell her what it was.

They pulled into the dealership and Cheryl asked, "What are we picking up here?" Dave laughed and the two walked over to the salesman who handed Dave the keys to the new RV saying, "I truly believe that this will bring you enjoyment for years to come." Dave took his wife over to the RV and opened the door for her to look inside which looked like a home with a kitchen, dining area, bedroom and a shower and bathroom. Dave said, "I will not be signing a new employment contract. This is for us to getaway and do all the things we denied ourselves over the decades. It is now our time."

The first thing that Dave put into the RV was the picture of Robin that had hung wherever he hung his hat. It was hung on the wall of the middle room. Cheryl was okay with the picture as she knew that Robin never posed a threat to her. The bond between Dave and Robin transcended sexual attraction.

Dave wrote his resignation letter and walked it to the office of the CEO. He handed it to Mr. Watson saying, "I will cherish every minute that I spent with this organization and will stay on until you find a suitable replacement. This position requires a special talent to lead a non-traditional law enforcement agency. I would be willing to write the job advertisement, if you would like.

Children's conducted a national search for a new director and received resumes from all over the country. Dave was tasked to reduce the applicants to five and those would receive a personal interview.

***

Dave and Cheryl left Cincinnati on a tour of the United States. They drove northeast through Pittsburgh, Philadelphia, D.C. and into New York. They attached the car to the rear so they could park the RV and cruise the cities. They attended a Broadway show in New York. They would stop to sleep at Interstate rest areas or RV parks where they could re-charge the batteries and hook into the sewage system. From New York the two went down the Eastern seaboard, passing through Virginia Beach and the North Carolina outer banks, before driving through Georgia and into Florida. They moved west through New

Orleans and into Dallas and Houston. From there, they went through New Mexico and into the southern tip of California. They followed the Pacific Ocean into Los Angeles and then moved east to Las Vegas. They passed through Denver and Oklahoma City and then went to St. Louis. The final leg of the trip went to Chicago and then Indianapolis before returning to Cincinnati. The quality time spent together cemented a marriage that has lasted almost forty years.

When they arrived home Cheryl suggested that they sell the house and become nomads living in the RV. Dave countered with buying one-half acre in a rural area and putting a concrete foundation in the center with electric, water and sewer hookups to use when they returned. They found a piece of property just east of Cincinnati. It would also provide them a mailing address.

They decided to go to Washington, D.C., but this time with a purpose. They would go to the Law Enforcement Memorial to see the Wall of Heroes and find Robin's name engraved on the granite wall. They left D.C. and drove to Charlotte to see the world famous race track, then went south to Charleston, South Carolina to see the naval base. They drove west to Atlanta and then north to Memphis and Nashville before heading back to their new property

Dave installed a gravel driveway to the cement block and detached the car before pulling it onto the slab and connecting the utilities. It would stay there until they were ready for the next trip.

The two were sitting outside the RV looking up at a clear sky and a full moon. Dave thought about Robin and could see her sitting in her place in Heaven looking down and telling him

"You have done well, my friend. Well done!"

CPSIA information can be obtained
at www.ICGtesting.com
Printed in the USA
LVHW071410170623
750063LV00001B/173